Little John and
Plutie

Pat Edwards

Published by The Trumpet Club
a division of Bantam Doubleday Dell Publishing Group, Inc.
666 Fifth Avenue, New York, New York 10103

ISBN: 0-440-84190-9

Reprinted by arrangement with Houghton Mifflin Company
Printed in the United States of America
January 1990

10 9 8 7 6 5 4 3 2 1
OPM

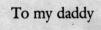
To my daddy

1

The train from Memphis was late. Both mules shivered their hides and stomped to rid themselves of the gnats swarming in the late afternoon sun. It would be night before long. John's hands were sweaty on the reins that Haze was letting him hold. He knew his father would be on that train and would drive the wagon home, but he couldn't help wondering, What if — What if something had happened and he wasn't on it? What then? John knew he would have to be the one to walk in front in the dark and carry the lantern and just hope he and Haze could find their way back home.

"You think maybe some holdup men stopped the train, Haze?" he asked the big black man on the seat beside him.

"Little John, you got more worry in your head for your size than any child I ever did see," said Haze. "You a natural born, big-time worrier. That train just a slowpoke. Take a heap of coal shoveling to keep it puffing along, and Memphis be a long way off from

Crawford. No cause for you to think up trouble happening to your papa."

John sat quiet for a minute and then said, "Supper's gonna be ruint. Mama'll be mad."

"Boy, your mama gonna be so pleased to see your papa step his foot across that porch she ain't gonna mind if supper set for a while. Ease your mind some and go yonder and fetch us a drink." He held out a tin cup and nodded toward the pump at the side of the little building that served as a railroad station. John handed the reins to Haze, climbed down, and headed for the pump on the other side of the tracks, but his mind wasn't easy. He pumped the handle until water spurted, then leaned over to drink before he filled the cup. He wondered if the men slouched against the side of the building were watching as he carried it back and wondered if he should have asked permission.

Haze drank the water in loud gulps, wiped his mouth with the back of his hand, and said, "Crawford got mighty fine drinking water. I could use me another little sip."

John thought Haze was probably keeping him busy so as to take his mind up and make the time pass, but he took the cup and went back to the pump. One of the men standing nearby called to him.

"You there, boy, whatcha name?"

John looked all around to make sure he was who the man was talking to and then answered, "John

Beaumont Greer's my name. It's all right if I use this pump, ain't it?"

"I reckon," was the answer. Then, "You that nigger's water boy?"

"No, sir," he said, his eyes on the mud around the pump and his face turning red. He was sorry he'd said "sir" to the snickering man. John thought about dumping the water in the cup on the ground and running back to the wagon, but he knew he'd just have to sit there with the men watching him.

"It's for me," he said, and lifting the cup to his mouth, he drank it all.

"Ain't you scared of getting nigger germs, boy?" another man asked and hooted. "Watch out, now. Nigger germs'll turn you black."

John walked slowly back to the wagon, kicking at the dried tufts of grass. He stood looking down the tracks for a long time before he could face Haze and hand him back the empty cup. He hated the men. He wished he'd brought the water. Said yes, he was the water boy. Made a joke of it. But when he got back to the wagon, Haze just put the cup under the board that served as a seat and said, "Never mind, Little John. Too much water bloats you anyhow."

"Sure does," said John, feeling about to pop and needing to go behind the bushes, but there weren't any. And another worry was starting to get to him. Germs. He wasn't so dumb as to think Haze's germs would turn him black, but his mama made a lot of fuss over watching out for germs, making him wash his hands just about every time she looked at him, not letting him use her glass if she had a cold or anything. He wondered if he might catch something awful from drinking out of that cup. It didn't make good sense. Haze looked strong and healthy. Nothing to catch from him. It was dumb to worry about it.

But when John was real little — only five or so — he got started thinking something terrible was about to happen to him. That was because three different people who used to be in his family weren't there anymore — his grandpapa and both of his brothers. All he knew then was that they got put into holes in the ground and they weren't ever going to come back.

One Sunday when they went to Riley and put flowers on his brothers' side-by-side graves, he had noticed that there was just the right amount of space left for one more little one before you got to his grandpapa's big grave. It looked like they were saving that place for somebody just his size.

His grandpapa had been the first to go. John's memory of him was hazy, just that he clumped when he walked because he'd lost a leg in the Civil War, and that he picked John up one time and carried him back to see the machinery that printed out the news every week in his shop in Riley.

Next there was Bentley, his nine-year-old brother who was old enough to ride on a mule all the way to the schoolhouse. When he got back home, he would teach John the things he had learned that day, taught

4

him to read some and taught him how much fun numbers could be. On the farm there was nobody to play with but each other and Lucy, an old hound dog, so it was lonesome after the mule bucked Bentley off on the way home one afternoon and whammed him up against the railing on the iron bridge. John never cared as much for doing numbers after that.

It wasn't long before the new baby brother came. They named him James and called him Spud because he was bald as a potato. He didn't last long enough to stop being a baby. A mule was what got him, too. He'd just started knowing how to walk and he wobbled up to one of the plowing mules out by the barn and whacked at its rear end with a stalk of sugar cane. You shouldn't ever walk up behind a mule even if you're a grown man.

After that his father wouldn't talk to anybody for a long time and once he got falling down drunk from whiskey. His mother had cried a whole lot back then and had fussed over John when he just had a cold or a stomachache. Sometimes at night she would wake him up trying to find out whether he was breathing or not.

He used to be scared prickly at night by imagining that there was a lion under his bed waiting to gobble him up when he had to go use the slop jar in the corner. Other times he would tell himself that a gorilla was hiding behind the barn waiting for him to walk by. Once in a while he would think about being carried down the aisle of the church in a box with honeysuckle all over the top. There'd be sniffing and sobbing and his mother would say to somebody, "This hurts the most of all of them. This is the hardest to bear."

Now John was as old as Bentley had been and nothing else really bad had happened. He'd stayed out of that space in the graveyard, at least. His mother had gone back to laughing once in a while and his father took up talking again, but with more cussing than there used to be. He kept trying to get a good crop of cotton, but one year the rain would be too heavy and the river would rise and swamp everything. The following year he'd say the rain was too skimpy. And the year after that the dratted weevils came and chewed up the bolls. There never was a chance to get ahead.

Early that spring his father had said they were doing so poorly with their little piece of cotton land that he'd decided he could make better money buying and selling mules. He liked mules better than horses, he said. With their big floppy ears and stringy tails, they might not be as pretty, but they were stronger. They didn't eat too much and they didn't seem to mind sizzling hot weather or flies. So he sold off a piece of their land and took off for Memphis with the money, headed for a place where he heard they were selling at a good price. Now John and Haze sat waiting for him to come home, and it seemed like it was taking forever.

As John was about to climb back onto the wagon seat, he heard a train whistle hooting a long way off and he grinned at Haze. "It's coming. That ole slow poke is finally getting itself on down the track."

"You go take you a look," said Haze. "I best stay here and mind the team."

A dark plume from the smokestack streamed across the evening sky as the train roared closer. Puffs of white steam hissed from around the cowcatcher, the V-shaped front of the engine that could clear the tracks of anything that dared to get in its way. John whispered the name his father had used, "locomotive," as the powerful pistons slowed and the train clanged to a stop. Locomotive was just the right name for it. Riding on one was about the grandest thing that could happen to a person. Last week when his daddy got on board and waved from the window, John had been mighty proud of him.

Now he ran along the edge of the track trying to get a glimpse inside so he'd know which of the two coaches his daddy would step down from, but the setting sun reflected in the windows and he couldn't see. A lady and a little girl took a long time getting off the first car. Three or four men came behind them, but none of them was his daddy. He ran to the door of the other car, but the conductor was already picking up the little step stool he put down so people could get off. Then up at the first car he saw two men helping somebody to the ground, holding on to his arms and then handing down his coat and hat.

"Daddy!" John cried, running toward his father, whose face was pale and shiny with sweat.

"Well, now, here's my boy come to meet me," he said with a little laugh, swaying slightly. "I'll be fine now, gentlemen. I'm much obliged to you."

John noticed that his daddy didn't have his grip. He turned to holler at the men to wait, but the train had already started to move.

Right at first, John thought that his father was sick, but as he put out his hand to steady him he smelled whiskey and knew that drunk was what he was.

"I'm just feeling out of sorts, son. Don't know what come over me." His hand was heavy and hot on John's shoulder. "Can't tell you how good it is to be back. How's Mama?"

"She's fine," John answered. "She rested a lot, like you said. She felt the baby kicking yesterday. Did you get some mules?"

"Well, yes and no," his father said, the words coming slower and slurred. "It's what you might call a long story." By the time they had reached the wagon, his knees sagged and John and Haze had to lift him into the back. Haze took off his own shirt and wadded it up for a pillow.

"Look like you plum wore yourself out up yonder, Mr. Joe. You just take your rest back here and leave everything to Little John and me. We get you home pretty soon."

So it turned out that before they got there, John did have to walk through the black of night carrying the lantern, but it didn't scare him the way he had imagined it would. He walked fast, pushing the darkness out of the road, with the mules snuffling right behind and strange noises coming from the underbrush beyond the circle of light. Haze sang little snatches of a song about "Come Jubilee Time," humming the part he didn't know the words to, and they found the way back without any wrong turns at all.

2

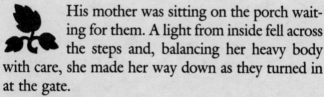 His mother was sitting on the porch waiting for them. A light from inside fell across the steps and, balancing her heavy body with care, she made her way down as they turned in at the gate.

"My goodness, you all are mighty late. Supper's a pure loss," she called. Then as she got closer her voice went tight. "And how come it's Haze driving, Joseph?"

"He just a mite poorly, Miss Eva." Haze tried to ease her. "He be all right in a little bit."

His daddy sat up and blinked. Brushing himself off as the wagon came to a stop, he called out in a hearty voice, "Now don't you worry, sugar. I took kind of woozy, is all. It's nothing to concern yourself over. I sure appreciate it, Haze — you taking the reins for me thata way."

John wished he could keep it from happening. Keep his mother from getting close enough to smell the whiskey. He had a crazy notion to fall down suddenly right there so she would run to him instead of his father, but it was too late. She had reached her husband and gone stiff and silent. Then she said softly, "I don't believe it. I swear to God I don't believe it." She turned, took the lantern from John, and handed it to Haze, then made her way back to the house, leaning on John's shoulder as heavily as his father had earlier.

The men went on around to unhitch the mules and he could hear his father being sick out by the barn. His mother put a plate of cold chicken pie in front of him and poured him a glass of milk. John tried to eat, but his mother's silence and his father's retching took away the hunger he had felt earlier. He had to force himself to swallow.

"You want some rice pudding?" she asked when he was done.

"No'm, I had aplenty."

"Get yourself to bed then," she said. "You must be worn to a frazzle, having to walk all that way." She kissed his forehead and he went off to his room, mostly glad to go and shut himself away, although some part of him wanted to be there when his father came in.

On hot nights John usually left his door open to pull the air in through the window, but he closed it that night. He undressed in the dark, throwing his pants and shirt on the floor, and got into bed in his underwear. The voices that came from the kitchen were muffled. He was too tired to try to make them out. His feet and legs ached. The voices turned shrill, and he started to say out loud the prayer he used to say when he was little, "Now I lay me down to sleep, I pray Thee, Lord, my soul to keep. If I should die before I wake, I pray Thee, Lord, my soul to take. Amen." He kept saying it over and over, starting at the beginning as soon as he got to amen, until he fell asleep.

He woke early. A catbird was making a fuss outside his window and it was still cool. Somebody was moving around on the other side of the house, but he couldn't tell by the sound which one of them it was. He hoped it was his daddy so he could get the straight of what happened about the mules.

He pulled on the pants he had worn the day before, opened the door, and headed for the outhouse, cutting his eyes around trying to see who it was that was stirring about. When he came back his daddy was there on the back steps waiting for him, his hair damp and a towel around his neck.

"Morning, son," he said. "Rest well?"

"Yes, sir. You feel all right?"

"Well — " he paused and squinted out across the fields, "I could say everything was fine and dandy, but you'd know and I'd know I'd be telling a lie. I'm feeling like I ate me a supper of tin cans." He sat down on the steps. "I want to say how much I appreciate what you did for me last night, son. It's a comfort knowing how you can take ahold."

"It was Haze did the driving," was all John could think of to say. Lucy came around the corner of the house greeting them with a hoarse little bark. She'd been old when Bentley was alive and by now she moved with early morning stiffness. John sat down beside his daddy so the dog could lick his face. He hoped his father wouldn't speak about being drunk.

"I ran into a little trouble — no, I guess it was pretty big trouble, son — while I was gone. What happened was, I'd done a whole lot of looking at mules. Traipsed from one end of town to the other. I wanted to make sure I was getting the best for my money. Finally, day before yesterday, I was satisfied. Thought I'd picked the cream of the crop. I was aiming to buy ten in all and have 'em shipped down by paddle boat."

He let out a long wavery sigh and rubbed the back of his neck.

"I was feeling mighty fine. I'd made all the arrangements with the shipping company, even paid up for part of the boat charge. The rest I was to give on delivery. All I had left to do was to go on over to the stockyard, get my ten mules marked, and pay up for them."

All of a sudden John felt like he knew how it was all going to come out.

"I was feeling mighty fine that night," his father

repeated. "I was bone tired, but I felt the deal had gone well and so I stepped into a — a drinking place. To celebrate, you might say — celebrate the fact that I'd been able to handle something I didn't know too much about. You know I never was a mule trader before, son. I was trying a new line of endeavor. I wasn't exactly a hundred percent sure I could do it, you see. I wasn't easy about going, putting up in a hotel and all. But it looked like I had it in the bag. It was something to celebrate. You understand?"

John nodded.

"So . . . well, I treated myself to a little refreshment my last night there. Seemed like there was nothing so terrible about doing that. I can tell you it was good to have somebody to talk to without having to worry about the other fellow outsmarting you. Good to feel you could let down your guard. People in such places enjoy bragging to one another. And I was moderate. I didn't overdo. You'd have had no cause to be ashamed, son."

His daddy seemed to expect him to say something, but John was having a hard time imagining him in there having a good time, laughing and bragging, having fun.

"However," his daddy said, hard and dragged out so you could tell the bad part was coming, "when I got myself dressed back at the hotel yesterday morning and felt for my money roll, well, there wasn't anything there but the change in my pocket. Some lowlife scoundrel had lifted my wallet. Likely somebody who had acted friendly and had likely given me a pat on the back while he snuck it out."

His daddy squeezed his mouth and eyes shut, hiccupped a sob, and slammed a fist into his palm. John had never seen him cry before. Not even after Bentley and Spud died. His shoulders jerked and he sounded strangled and funny. John wanted to hit him and make him stop.

Instead he asked, "Why didn't you get the sheriff to go after whoever it was and get it back?"

"No use, son. That money was long gone by then."

"You could have tried, seems like."

His father looked at him, wiped his face on the towel, and took a deep breath. "Now you're sounding like your mama. Well, I tried. I did try, but nothing came of it." Then, "It would take a braver man than me to come back here and tell your mama cold sober what happened."

"You came back drunk," John blurted out, his own eyes suddenly starting to fill.

"I just thought to have a little something to ease me. I still had my ticket for coming back, see. I'd bought one for both ways before I left. So I could get on the train. But the thought of walking into this house empty-handed and a fool to boot . . . well, I couldn't face up to it. What loose change I had was enough to buy me a bottle to take along. I thought to take just enough to ease me. But the closer I got the worse I felt."

Neither one of them said anything for a long time,

and John heard his mother moving about in the bedroom.

"I can't tell you how sorry I am, son. I don't know how I can make it up to you and your mama, God help me. But maybe this can teach you some sense, anyhow. Whiskey can't fix things a-tall! Just harms. Remember that, will you?"

"Yes, sir," he answered. "Don't feel bad." But he couldn't think of any good reason why not.

His daddy reached out and rumpled John's hair, the way he did to show he liked him. "Thank you, son. Hearing you say that means a lot to me. I appreciate it. Reminds me. I bought a little something to bring back to you, but I went and left it in the grip."

"What happened to it, to the grip?"

"Well, the hotel folks had to keep it when I couldn't pay them what I owed. I'm sorry. I have to keep on saying that, looks like. It was a harmonica I bought you."

"That's all right. I wouldn't know how to play on one anyhow."

"A smart fellow like you could learn in no time. Why, you could have taught me after you got good at it. Wouldn't that be something, us playing tunes together?"

John thought he'd never heard his daddy say so much at one time before. He remembered how he hadn't said much of anything but yes and no right after Spud got kicked. Now it seemed like feeling awful made him just keep on talking, not able to stop. But not about what was bothering John. Not about what was going to happen next.

In the spring his daddy had sold off most of the cotton land, everything except their house and the little shack where Haze and his wife lived, the barn and what was going to be the mule lot, and a little piece of land for raising corn and vegetables. The money was to stake the trip to Memphis to buy the first mules and then to add on to the barn as they got more of them. Part of the money was in the bank at Riley, but most of it was in the pocket of some low-down thief that probably looked like those men at the train station in Crawford, the kind who most likely drank whiskey every day. So he asked, "What's gonna happen now, Daddy?"

"Hard to say, son. I'll have to think on it once I get my brains to working right."

"How you aim to do that?" he asked, putting an edge of sass to it.

"Well," his daddy grinned. "A cup of coffee might be a start."

While his daddy was splitting kindling to start a fire in the cookstove, John went out to the barn to see if Haze was milking yet. He'd been giving John lessons. He found him sitting on a stool squirting warm milk into a pail.

"Somebody stole his money," he told Haze,

scratching Betsy between her ears. "He never got the mules."

"Is that a fact!" Haze's eyes widened and he shook his head. "I sho' hate to hear it. Mr. Joe had his mind set on mule trading — gonna make y'all good money. Miss Eva take it pretty hard?"

"I guess," said John. "I ain't seen her yet this morning. Daddy and me talked all about it. He feels awful. He craves a cup of coffee."

"I seen him setting out there before it was good daylight. I knowed he was troubled. Dancie got a pot going. You go ask her for a cup and take it to him while I finish up here. And take this along." He poured some of the foamy milk into a smaller pail. "She like fresh milk in her coffee."

Haze and Dancie had lived on the Greer place ever since John could remember, helping to chop cotton and pick it, doing chores. Now that the land had been sold, Haze tended the garden and hired out for day work now and then. Dancie made clothes. She was good at it. Ladies would drive out from Riley in their buggies to have her make pretty dresses.

She opened the door before he got to the end of the path back to their shack. She was a woman not much for smiling, not easy to be with like Haze. Dancie always made him feel he was interrupting something. She never asked him to sit down or to tell her what he'd been up to. If Haze was there he might ask her to fix John a piece of bread and jelly, but she would never offer it on her own.

Now she said "Good morning," but without calling him by his name. If he hadn't brought the milk along he would have been bashful about asking for the coffee, but the cow belonged to his family, so he had a right.

"Here's some milk for you, Dancie. Haze said for you to let me have a cup of your coffee to take to my daddy. He's kinda ailing."

"Mm-hmm, I could let him have some," she said. "Just set the bucket there on the step." She turned and disappeared inside, returning in a moment with a pink glass cup not quite full. "You mind now you don't break my cup, and bring it back when he's done finished."

He almost said, "Yes'm," though he certainly knew you weren't supposed to say "ma'am" or "sir" to a colored person. He walked carefully down the path, taking a deep breath of the good coffee smell that was mixing with the smells from the barn and the honeysuckle along the fence. He wished Dancie had put the coffee into a jelly jar or something not so likely to spill. He wished Dancie liked him more.

His father had just got the cookstove going and was glad to get the coffee. Said it hit the spot. His mother still hadn't come out of the bedroom. When they had cooked some grits, his daddy spooned up a bowlful, dropped a pat of butter into it, and set it on a tray along with a cup of tea.

"How about you take this in to her," his daddy said. "Breakfast in bed'll do her good."

"She's not in bed," John said. He could hear drawers slamming shut harder than necessary.

"Well, my guess is she'd enjoy eating more without the sight of me this morning. Go on."

When his mother opened the door she looked down at John and the tray. "What's this?" she asked.

"Daddy thought you might rather have breakfast in bed," he said, holding his face up for a good-morning kiss, but noticing that what was going on in the room was packing up to go somewhere.

She cleared a spot on top of the bureau and stood stirring the melting butter in. "Ask your daddy to fix you some eggs. I'm planning to get Haze to drive you and me in to Gran's house later today. You'll need a stick-to-your-ribs kind of breakfast."

"Don't you want some eggs, too?" he asked, uneasy about asking the question in the front of his mind, the question of how mad she was at his daddy. She shook her head.

"And after you finish we have to pack you up some clothes."

"Daddy had to leave his grip at the hotel," he said, to let her know he'd been told all about it.

"We can do without," she answered, spooning in a mouthful of grits. "And tell your daddy to have Haze hitch the wagon up."

But his daddy wouldn't hear of her bouncing along in the wagon. For a good while she had been trying to have babies and kept losing them. This one was due in less than three months, but there was no stopping her going. So Haze rode over to Riley on a mule and hitched up Gran's buggy so she could come out to get them. Riley wasn't as far as Crawford, and they would be there in time for supper. For how long, nobody had said.

3

At midafternoon John sat waiting on the porch with Lucy nuzzling him, her long tail dragging and her ears limp. She seemed to know he was going off again. Yesterday his mother had to lock her in the barn to keep her from running down the road after the wagon. John had wanted to bring her along today but there was no room in the buggy. Anyway, she'd be better off where she was. Gran always accused Lucy of having fleas, but John thought she just scratched a lot because it was one of the few things she could do for fun now. She was pretty old and wasn't much for chasing rabbits anymore. Also, she let out a mournful howl when there was any kind of commotion, and town noises would have her making a racket all night.

When Gran and Haze drove up, John called to his father and they brought out the bundles of clothes for him and Mama, along with a basket of corn and squash from the garden. Gran started out not saying anything about what had happened and acted as if it was perfectly natural for somebody to leave home the day after her husband came back from a trip.

She held out her arms and John jumped up on the step of the buggy to get a hug that smelled of talcum powder and violet water. "How's my boy?"

"Just fine, Gran." That was what he always said. His father greeted her, a little stiffer, maybe, than he usually acted, but trying to pretend nothing was out of the ordinary.

"Afternoon, Miss Sally. Hot enough for you?"

"Welcome back, Joseph. How was your trip?" Neither one answered the other one's question. She went right on. "My, what splendid-looking vegetables you've grown. That cushaw squash . . . that's a beauty."

"Wouldn't you care to come take a little stretch before you turn right around?"

"Well, I s'pose." He took her arm as she eased herself to the ground. "I'm not as spry as a spring chicken and neither is Maud here." She patted the horse's flank. "While Haze gives her a drink I'll go in for a minute and see if I can hurry Eva along."

The mule Haze had ridden on the way over had been tied to the back of the buggy on the return trip. Haze undid him and headed off toward the barn. John didn't know what his mother had written in the note Haze took to Riley, but he was pretty sure she hadn't told the whole awful story. He stood with his father, who kept shifting things around in the buggy and checking the horse's harness. Finally he spoke.

"I want you to be specially nice to your mama, son.

23

She's mighty upset. It's a bad time for a woman to be upset, you know."

"Yeah, I reckon she's pretty mad. Prob'ly she's in there telling Gran all about what happened."

"I wouldn't be surprised."

John was pleased he and his father were sharing this thing. It felt like man talk. "I'll watch out for her. How long are we going for?" Now he was able to ask.

"Lord knows, son. If it looks like I'm needed, you try to get me word, if you can."

John's stomach went funny. "Mama would never let me ride by myself." Since what had happened to Bentley, it had been a firm rule that he was not to get on a horse or mule until he was at least ten years old, which was a good six months off.

"You could maybe get somebody to bring a note. Or if worse came to worst . . . in a pinch . . . well, it won't. Don't you worry, son. I'm blowing this up out of all proportion. She'll come back."

John's stomach felt worse. He'd tried not to let himself think about not coming back at all, about staying there in town permanently.

Haze brought the bucket of water for Maud and gave her a handful of hay. He teased John about his milking lessons. "Shame you got to go now when you finally starting to get the hang of it a little bit. Ain't gonna be no place at Miss Sally's for you to practice what you learnt. Reckon I'll have to start you all over from scratch." That sounded hopeful to John, like they'd be back for sure.

"His grandmama will likely have him practicing the fiddle instead. Son, you remember your granddaddy's fiddle she keeps wrapped up in a silk cloth? You might start in on that while you're over there. Give you something to do. Playing the fiddle ought to keep his milking fingers in shape, Haze, don't you think?"

"It ain't the same, Mr. Joe. Milking be a whole different handling from anything else."

"Gran calls it a violin. She won't let me touch it until there's somebody to give me lessons." She'd showed it to him every time he went there and talked about him becoming a fine musician so they could all be proud of him someday. She was always going on about one thing or another he might do to make her proud.

The two women came out of the house then, and from the pinkish look on their faces John was sure a lot of talk had been going on.

"Joseph," said Gran, setting her sun hat back on her head, "I hear tell they're hiring hands for the big new Baptist church they're building over in Crawford. Not what you'd call a high-class job — they don't pay a whole lot, but something's better than nothing, don't you think?"

"I couldn't argue with you there, Miss Sally," he answered, his face, too, turning pink. He helped the women into the buggy, but without any kind of hugging good-byes. Then, after rumpling John's hair and patting him on the back, he stooped down to hold on to Lucy. All his mother said was, "I'd appreciate it if you'd send Haze over in a few days to see if I forgot anything we need."

Haze took hold of Maud's harness, leading her around to face toward Riley, and stepped back to wave them off. John sat between the two women and Gran gave a tap to the horse with her buggy whip so that they went lickety-split down the road, much faster than you could ever go in a wagon. A little later she let him drive for a while so she could hold her handkerchief against her nose to keep out the dust the horse kicked up, but she took the reins back before they got to the bridge where Bentley got bucked off. His mother always closed her eyes at that spot. Every time he passed, John tried to imagine how it must have felt to be Bentley. Whether he'd known it was his last look at the willow trees along the bank as he went whizzing through the air. Which exact spot on the railing he hit.

"Did you say a little prayer for your brother?" his mother asked with a sigh as she took his hand in hers and held it.

"Yes, ma'am," he answered, and quickly in his head he asked God to bless Bentley. But as far as he could tell, from what everybody had said, both Bentley and Spud were safe in Jesus' arms on the other side of the River Jordan, wherever that was, in Heaven, waiting to welcome the rest of them over to that side where nothing bad ever happened. He figured it was those still on this side who needed watching out for, who had hard times to put up with.

As if she were reading his thoughts, Gran began to sing "Shall We Gather at the River," one of her favorites. She made it sound bouncy and almost like a dance — "the beau-ti-ful, the beau-ti-ful ri-ver!" At the very end she reached into her skirt pocket and brought out a little bag of the hard candies with swirls inside he'd always called winding balls. He took a cherry-flavored one and his mother picked lemon, but Gran declared she'd rather sing and started in on "There's a Land That Is Fairer Than Day." The sun that was shining into John's eyes right then was so bright that it hurt and he tried to imagine how he'd manage in Heaven if it was any brighter there. He wondered if people who drank whiskey went to Heaven. If not, they'd have to go to the bad place, to Hell. The idea of his father going down there was crazy. He'd never believe a crazy thing like that. He wished he was back home with him and Haze and Lucy right now. And he'd a hundred times rather learn to milk than to play any dumb violin. Still, at the same time he really kind of liked the way Gran and his mama treated him — like he was special some-how. It seemed he could be two different people, the one he was right now, sucking on a winding ball and enjoying a buggy ride, and the one he'd been back there, man-talking with his daddy.

After a while his mother, looking out across the

27

fields where the cotton bolls were beginning to show white, said, "Wouldn't you know he'd give up on farming just the year when the crops are doing so well!"

"That's your Joseph, daughter. Well, the Lord moves in mysterious ways. We can't know what He has in mind for him."

John got the feeling that Gran wasn't a bit sorry to be taking them away from his daddy, that she'd be pleased to have them all to herself for a while. She had a way of talking friendly with everybody, but he could tell she always looked down a little on his father, who never had a whole lot in the way of schooling. Gran liked to talk about how well educated her husband had been, how well he had run the town's newspaper, and how he had been crazy about books and music. Sometimes she would read John pieces out of the paper he'd written and say, "Just listen to the turn of that phrase." And she'd read it all over again. He never heard her brag much on his father. Except maybe today when she said the cushaw squash was fine-looking. He was careful never to let his daddy know that he enjoyed the way Gran paid him so much attention and gave him little treats and all. He acted like it was something he just had to put up with. It was like there were sides to be on.

"A job helping out with the construction over there in Crawford might be the very thing for him," said Gran.

"But, Mama, it wouldn't lead anywhere. What's he

going to do — lay bricks the rest of his days?"

"I don't know, Eva. Maybe so. The world has to have bricklayers. Maybe that's the true level of his talents."

"Mama! You know that's not true!" Sometimes when Gran pushed too far, his mother would flare up and take his daddy's side. "Joe's got plenty of sense in his head. He's got lots of ability. But he's sure made a mess of things this time. What I couldn't take — could not *abide* — was his coming home in that state." Then, as if he hadn't known, she turned to John and said, "I'm sorry to tell you, honey, but it was whiskey that was ailing your father last night."

It seemed easier to play dumb. "Wasn't he sick, Mama?"

"No, my dear," Gran said. "He was drunk. You're old enough to understand. That's what drinking does to a man. Makes him sick and crazy. Irresponsible. Why, your brother James might be riding along with us today if it weren't for liquor."

"Mama, don't say that!" his mother cried. "You don't know it was like that."

"Well, there *had* been drinking going on that day, daughter. John's man enough to look at things straight on, aren't you, son?"

"He did get drunk, but that was after," John said. "I saw him that time, but it was after."

"So say some," said Gran.

"Just hush now, Mama," his mother said. "We've been over this and over it. That horrible day. But it

29

was on account of everybody getting food poisoning like that. You can't put it on Joe, what happened to Spud."

There'd been a family reunion that summer day with kinfolks on his father's side coming from a long way off, Uncle Walter and his little girl, Stella, and Uncle Oscar, who was close to ninety, and eight or ten others. His daddy enjoyed showing off both his children, carrying Spud around and trying to make him giggle or say "Papa," and getting John to amaze everybody by adding numbers in his head. Then folks started feeling queasy. Some were throwing up or getting stomach cramps. They thought the heat had likely got to the potato salad and made it go bad. Somebody said the awful word *ptomaine*, and at that old Uncle Oscar stretched right out on the ground and took to moaning. Everybody was either running for the outhouse or busy seeing to the old man, and never noticed that Spud had wandered out to where the mules were. John himself was feeling all right but was hiding under the house in the cool soft dirt with his hands over his ears to shut out the sick sounds and Uncle Oscar's pitiful moans, when his mother gave a scream so loud he couldn't shut it out — a scream he kept hearing in his dreams for a long time. Uncle Oscar got all right, but Spud didn't. He died the next morning.

Now the sound of his father being sick last night came to him and connected with what he remembered of three years ago. Maybe Papa really had been drunk then, too, and had been the cause of Spud getting killed. Maybe you couldn't trust him. Maybe, one way or another, he did always mess things up. Maybe, John thought, he himself might be better off just being the one special person he was with the womenfolks.

"I can tell you one thing," he said. "I ain't never going to drink any whiskey as long as I live."

"I'm *not ever* going to drink it," his mother corrected him. Then she squeezed his hand and said to Gran, "Thank God for this boy."

"Yes, indeed. He's our hope and our comfort." She let him drive most of the way back to Riley and let him keep the whole bag of winding balls.

4

Gran had a couple of boarders. She hated to have to do it — it felt common, he'd heard her say once — but she couldn't manage without the money after Grandpapa died, so she hired Haze's mama, Bella, to do the cooking and help with one of the boarders, a very old man who used to be a schoolmaster and who took a lot of tending to because he was nearly blind and always having some kind of ailment. Mr. Duff was his name, and there was a camphor and medicine smell all through the house from his being in it. The other boarder was Miss Rennie, a maiden lady who worked at the post office.

They were there, waiting for their supper, the summer evening that John and his mother arrived. At least they were out of sight when he and Gran brought in the load of bundles and put them in the room he'd have to share with his mother. There was a big four-poster bed and a cot by the window that he used whenever they came visiting. Gran kept hoping she'd get a schoolteacher to rent that room, but so far she hadn't had any luck. There were places closer to the schoolhouse, some with bathrooms right inside the house.

"Now you lie right down, daughter. You need a good rest after all that jouncing about. John and I'll get supper on the table and call you when it's ready. It'll be a cold supper since Bella has the day off to go to a baptizing for one of her multitude of grandchildren. Stretch yourself out here now. John, help your mother get comfy and then come give me a hand in the kitchen." She went on downstairs and he folded up the bedspread after his mother lay down and turned her face toward the wall with the old brown water stain on it. When he walked around to put the spread away in the cedar chest, he could see a tear ooze from his mother's closed eyes and roll down to drop off the edge of her cheek. It went through his head that he'd seen both of his parents cry that day. Then he tiptoed out and closed the door, as if he thought she was already asleep.

In the dining room he set the silverware with great care, placing each piece exactly the same distance from the edge, trying not to think about all the crying. He put fresh napkins in the napkin rings for his mother and himself and put Gran's and Miss Rennie and Mr. Duff's used ones beside their plates. He wished Bella had been there instead of off somewhere. She had a soft easy laugh and could cheer up the house, which suddenly seemed strange and lonesome, like he didn't belong there at all. To make things worse, he caught

33

a whiff of the sick, old man smell from Mr. Duff and then got a glimpse of Miss Rennie going out on the back porch to fill her pitcher. He ducked behind the china cabinet. She was a dried-up sort of lady whose mouth looked sour, as if she'd spent the day at the post office licking stamps.

Gran brought in a plate of ham sandwiches along with a dish of sliced tomatoes and cucumbers. There was a bowl of cornbread and milk for Mr. Duff. She tinkled a little silver bell that meant supper was ready and went to get his mother. He wondered if she would come to the table at all or if she had cried herself sick, but she came out smiling a big smile for Miss Rennie and Mr. Duff and pretended she'd caught a terrible cold that made her eyes runny and her nose stuffy.

"John here will just have to shake hands for the both of us," she said, trying to sound bright and perky, giving him a little shove toward where they were standing politely behind their chairs, waiting. "Nobody better get close to me this evening."

"Well, I *am* susceptible," said Miss Rennie, edging her chair a little closer to Mr. Duff's as they sat down. Gran bowed her head and said her usual blessing, "Lord, make us grateful for what we are about to receive. Amen."

Mr. Duff said "Amen" too in his quavery voice and started in on his bread and milk, but Miss Rennie, as she helped herself to a sandwich, had to ask, right off, "Well, I'm dying to know. How did Mr. Greer fare on his trip up to Memphis? Did those sharp Tennessee traders eat him up alive?" She seemed to think that was pretty funny and laughed with what sounded like hiccups. Nobody answered so she changed her tune. "I'm sure he never let them get the best of him, did he?"

John looked at his mother, but she had taken a big bite of sandwich and just raised her eyebrows to show everybody that she couldn't answer right then. Gran took over. "Oh, well, we won't know that, of course, until he gets back, Miss Rennie."

"Oh? I thought you said he was due to come back yes-tiddy. I believe I did tell you about how I have trouble digesting cucumbers, Miz Beaumont."

"No," said Gran, cool as a cucumber herself. "He was detained. Try a little vinegar on them. That helps." John was so surprised he swallowed wrong and had to go around the table for his mother to give him little slaps between his shoulder blades. He couldn't believe his ears. That Gran had told an out-and-out lie. Actually, his mother had, too, but pretending you had a cold wasn't as bad as saying something hadn't happened when it had. He wondered what the punishment was for a lie like that.

Gran changed the subject right quick by starting to talk about how well Bella's grandson Pluto was doing. He was only twelve years old, but he helped out around the big livery stable downtown where Maud was kept along with a lot of other town horses. Since Grandpapa wasn't around to ride anymore, Gran had sold off the pasture land where the horse used to be kept and now paid the livery people to look after her. Pluto would give her a workout every so often and came to hitch her up whenever Gran needed to go somewhere in the buggy.

John had heard about Pluto but he never had met him. He used to live a good way off, but back in the spring there was some talk about his sassing a white man or getting into some kind of trouble, so Bella went down and brought him back to stay until it blew over.

"He's just good as gold about coming by here to see what needs doing. Brings in stove wood and takes out the ashes — whatever."

"Accompanies me to the outhouse upon occasion," said Mr. Duff — the first words he'd spoken besides "Amen" since he sat down.

"That's so," said Gran, acting pleasant, as if outhouse talk was perfectly good table conversation. "When you're unduly indisposed, he does do that. I find him very willing and polite myself. And smart, too. A smart youngster."

"Too smart for his own good, I hear tell," said Miss Rennie, who thought she knew a lot about everything from overhearing all the remarks that were passed in the post office. "Is there something else coming?" Her plate was clean. Crusts and cucumbers and all had disappeared.

Gran got up and brought back a peach cobbler with a pitcher of cream and asked John to get saucers from the china cabinet.

"Isn't there any applesauce? I'm partial to apple-sauce," the old man said, sounding as if he might start to cry.

"No, now, Mr. Duff. You'll do fine with this. Just take your time and let the cream soak into the crust to get nice and soft. It's good and it's good for you." She talked to him like he was a little boy.

The cobbler *was* good — good and spicy — and John was thinking about asking for another helping when he happened to look over at his mother. She was sitting there just pushing sliced peaches around in the dish and tears were rolling down her cheeks a mile a minute. He had to say something to draw attention to himself before anybody noticed her.

"Can Pluto read, Gran? I could probably teach him if he can't. I was trying to teach Clem in school last winter, but he's backward. He couldn't get the hang of it." They were all looking at him. He felt dumb but he went on. "If Pluto's smart, I might could teach him."

There was a loud scraping sound as his mother pushed her chair back and got up, wiping her eyes with a soggy handkerchief and mumbling, "Excuse me — awful cold." But then the sobs burst through.

"You go lie down, honey. I'll save your dessert for later. A cold can certainly spoil an appetite," she said to Miss Rennie, who had turned to watch his mother go down the hall.

"Why, *feed* a cold and starve a fever is what I always heard. Is she all right?"

"Well, *can* he read or not?" Mr. Duff asked. "You never answered the boy. I should hate to see intelligence gone to waste. I was a teacher myself for nigh onto fifty years. Bet you didn't know that, son. That's a long time."

John did know. The old man told him that every single time he saw him.

"I'm not sure he cares about learning to read," Gran answered. "But there's lots of other things a colored child can benefit from learning to do. He's got a good head on his shoulders, I can tell you that." She kept on eating her cobbler with small careful bites, looking like she was determined to make this a pleasant meal, acting as if nothing was the matter.

John didn't want to be there. He remembered how it was back home. Not the times when his parents were mad at one another, but the good times when they sat around the supper table, Mama talking on about nothing much, with an easy feel to it. Sometimes they could be quiet for a long time and it was all right. He remembered how sometimes his daddy would go behind Mama's chair, put his arms around her to give her a big hug and say something silly like, "The good ole sweet mama. Ain't she the prettiest lady this side of the river, son?"

Again he felt pulled toward his daddy's side, the side he'd gone back on earlier in the afternoon when he'd said nobody would ever catch him drinking whiskey. After all, his grandmother didn't always tell the truth. She wasn't perfect.

When he was alone with her in the kitchen helping dry the supper dishes, she brought it up. "John, you heard me tell a little story to Miss Rennie in there this evening, didn't you?"

"Told a story" was what Gran said when she meant "lied." At least when she caught him at it. He nodded.

"Well, sometimes it's what you have to do to protect a loved one. Did you know that?" He shook his head. What she had always told him was God doesn't like it when you tell a story like that. It's a pain in the heart of Jesus.

"Your mother has had another cruel shock, after a whole string of heartaches that would have broken a weaker woman. I don't have to tell you that. She's come through the fire. She's stood by that man — by your father — beyond the call of duty. But she wasn't ready for Miss Rennie to ask her all about what happened in this present disaster. A person needs time for the wounds to start to heal before being called upon to exhibit them to anybody who asks to see. You understand that, don't you?"

"Yes'm. I guess."

"You and I have to smooth your mother's path in every way we can until she's stronger." She leaned over and took his chin in her dishpan-damp hand to look right into his eyes.

"You're the one she's counting on now."

Part of him wanted to pull away. He couldn't help wondering who was supposed to smooth his daddy's path. That man — she'd called him. He wondered if

39

Dancie had cooked him any supper. Dancie had never liked cooking for white folks. Would rather be a field hand or do the fancy sewing. But maybe she'd bring him something. Suddenly he remembered the coffee cup. He never took it back. She'd be mad.

"How would you like to go to school right here in Riley?" Gran asked him. A shiver ran down his back. His grandmother had often said it was a shame that a boy with brains as good as his had to go to the little one-room country school at Black Creek, that he couldn't have the advantage Bentley had here in town. Of course, she didn't want him riding back and forth every day either.

The Black Creek school was near enough for him to walk when the weather was good. His mama kept him home when it wasn't, and they would take turns reading out of some books she had when she was little. She'd make him practice his penmanship along the edges of old catalogues, making long rows of rolling *O*'s and sharp, even, up-and-down lines. So the teacher at Black Creek thought he was real bright. But the only one of the ten children there who was close to his age was Clem Croker, and he wasn't smart enough to get much past the ABC's. The teacher had about given up on him. For arithmetic John sat with Amelia Thompson and Hosie Reed, who were the oldest ones in the school and who winked at each other and passed notes and didn't care a lick about numbers. If he went to school in Riley, there'd likely be children in his grade a lot smarter than he was.

And he wouldn't know a single one of them.

"I reckon I ought to stay in Black Creek for a while," he said. "Who would see to Clem if I wasn't to go back?"

"Would you listen to that! If you aren't just about the best boy God ever let live! Always thinking of the other fellow that way. But sometimes, John Beaumont, you have to look out for your own welfare. A good education is mighty important." Gran went back to the dishwashing, shaking her head over how good he was, when he'd been thinking about himself all the time, thinking about being scared silly of a new place and strange people.

When they had finished in the kitchen, Gran went in to see about his mother while he took the dish towels out to hang in the back yard. Lightning bugs blinked in the dusk and he wandered over the grass grabbing at them, but only half trying. He followed one that flew toward the window where his mother was and heard Gran's I-know-I'm-right voice. "But you *have* given him chance after chance. You cannot throw your life away on somebody who doesn't have it in him to make a go of things."

John walked off a little way and lay down on the grass that was beginning to feel damp with evening dew. He lay watching for the first star, wondering if he himself had it in him to make a go of things. And he wondered if anybody had remembered to feed Lucy.

5

He met Pluto the next morning and liked him right off. John had stayed in bed late, pretending to be asleep so as not to be at the breakfast table with the others. He lay blinking at the brown water stain on the wall, trying to see how many things it looked like, until he heard Miss Rennie leave the house. When he walked into the kitchen, Bella made him feel she was tickled to see him and said, in a way that sounded like a compliment, "I declare, you gets more like your daddy every time I lay eyes on you." Then she fixed him a bowl of oatmeal and after that sent him out to see if there were any figs ripe yet.

As he started down the steep steps into the back yard a big mother hen clucked at her puffy little chicks scuttling between him and the tree, eyeing him to see what he was up to. He remembered falling into a chicken family like that once, remembered how the mother hen came at him while he was lying flat on his back, her wings all hunched up and her sharp beak bobbing at him. Ever since, he'd known to stay clear of chickens when they were watching out for their biddies. He sat down on the steps and waited for them to move on somewhere else.

Right then Pluto came around the corner of the house doing a kind of hopping jig and landed nearly on top of one of the soft, little peeping chicks. Sure enough, the fat hen fluffed up her feathers and headed for him. But Pluto spread his own elbows to match her wings, and the knees of his raggedy overalls pumped up and down as he and the chicken closed in on each other, threatening, nose to beak. The chicken moved off first, clucking angrily for her children to pick up their feet and follow.

Pluto straightened and jeered after her, turned, and saw John. "Have mercy! Who you?"

"John Beaumont Greer. This is my grandmama's house. I reckon you're Pluto."

"That's me! Leastwise that's what they tells me and I got no cause to think otherwise. What you doing here, John Bo?"

He liked being called a nickname. He liked the sound of it, too. "We come to visit. My mama and me."

"Y'all live out toward Crawford. I know. My uncle Haze live on your place, right?"

"He works for my daddy. Part-time now. You know Dancie?"

"I hear tell of her. We ain't met. You here for long, John Bo?"

"Oh, a while, I guess."

"You play mumbly peg?" asked Pluto, digging into his overall pocket.

"I don't s'pose I know how. Reckon you could show me?"

Pluto drew a circle with his big toe in a patch of bare ground, moved back three steps, and drew a straight line. Standing at the edge of it, he opened a pocket knife and held it out in the palm of his hand to be admired. The blade was nicked and a little rusty, but John sucked in his breath in approval.

"Watch now." Pluto took aim down the side of the blade, flexed his wrist several times, and the knife spun through the air and stuck straight up close to the middle of the circle.

"Hot dog! How you like that? Ain't that something!"

It surely was. John didn't think he'd ever in his life be able to do a thing like that. And his mother didn't like him fooling with knives anyhow.

"Want a try?" said Pluto, but before he could pass the knife to John, Gran appeared on the back porch.

"Good morning, Pluto."

"Morning, Miz Beaumont. How you feeling this morning?"

"Oh, can't complain. I see you've met my grandson."

"Yessum. I was 'bout to smarten him up a little bit along the line of mumbly peg, but you got something you want me to do — besides tending to Mr. Duff's convenience?"

That must be how Gran had taught Pluto to talk about emptying a slop jar. The others took their own out every morning if it had to be done, and rinsed it afterward at the pump before putting it away in the little cupboard in each room.

"I want you to take the washing down to Loreen for me later on today, but it will likely be afternoon before I get it all together. Do they need you at the stable this morning?"

"Yessum. They looking for me to show up."

"Well, Maud won't need a workout any time soon." The horse was tied to a hitching post near the shed where the buggy was kept. "She put in a good day's work yesterday, but I'd appreciate it if you'd take her on down there after you finish up here."

"Could he go with me?" Pluto nodded at John, who was pleased that the older boy wanted his company. "They ain't gonna mind. It's a couple of white children hangs around down there."

"They might not mind, but his mother might. If you care to go, John, you'll have to run ask her."

He found her sitting on the front porch with a pan of black-eyed peas in her lap. She was supposed to be shelling them for noontime dinner, but she was just staring off over the trees, her face blotched and puffy. She wouldn't let him go. There was no way to change her mind.

"Don't ask me that, John. A livery stable is the last place on the face of the earth I'd let you go right now. Just stay here in the yard. You understand me?"

On his way back through the house he met Pluto, who had put the clean convenience in Mr. Duff's room and was taking his big water pitcher out to fill it up. John walked with him to the pump.

"She won't let me. I'm sure sorry." Then, to let him know he wasn't a sissy mama's boy, he added, "Dad drat it!"

"Don't make no never mind. Big Mama done tole me what happen to y'all's little boys. It worry her mind for you to go around horses."

"It was mules that did it. Mules ain't nothin' but trouble."

"Me and mules gits along fine. Mr. Shumway down at the livery stable say I got a special way with 'em. I can get a mule to go what won't budge a smidgen for a grown man."

"My mama's making me wait until I'm ten to learn riding. That's next year. I betcha I'm the only boy my age in the whole county never been on any kind of four-legged critter. Makes me feel like a dumb baby."

"If you still be 'round here when you gets to be ten, I speck I could learn you how. See, I'm real good at explaining stuff." John thought it must be fine to feel so sure about what you could do.

"Ain't you going back to live with your family?"

"I might not. I likes it in Riley. Big Mama treats me nice. There's folks back there got it in for me."

46

"You go to school?"

"I went some. Not long."

"You know how to read?"

"Not a whole heap. What I can do is read and write my name. My name stands for god of the underworld. You know that?"

"You're named for the devil?" John asked.

"Naw, I don't think so. You ain't learned in school about Pluto?" John shook his head. "Pluto was a pretty powerful ole-timey god. I don't know too much about him myself, except how he could do most anything he took a mind to. I figured they got ail about him in books at the white folks school. Who you named for? Your daddy?"

"Uh-uh. It was my brother got his name, but he just went by the middle part, Bentley. I was named for my grandpapa, but it's the same name as Jesus' best friend in the Bible — John is."

When they went in to set the pitcher in Mr. Duff's washbowl, the old man was sitting in a chair looking drowsy and Gran was making up his bed.

"He cain't go, Miz Beaumont. I got to be running on."

"Well, I thought not. You can come back right after dinner. I'll have the washing tied up to go by then."

Gran went to help John's mother shell the peas and he went out to sit in the tattered old swing in the cedar tree where his mother had played when she was little. She hadn't had any brothers or sisters to play with either, and he wondered who had come over to push her in the swing and to have a good time with.

He was glad Pluto was coming back. He'd never really had a friend. Clem Croker was the closest thing to one and he didn't quite count. He would try to do whatever John told him to, but he couldn't even manage to play ticktacktoe without getting mixed up about whether he was *X*'s or *O*'s. Pluto was somebody he'd be mighty proud to have for a friend. He was somebody to have fun with and to learn things from, too . . . just the way he used to feel about Bentley. Maybe for turnabout, he could teach him how to read, the way Bentley did him. That ought to make Pluto like him and want to be his friend. Of course most colored people acted like they liked white people anyway, just because they were white. Except for Dancie. But sometimes he wondered why it should be like that. He wanted Pluto to like him, not just because he was white. Maybe, it was a curious thought, he could like him in spite of it.

Gran called to him not to swing so high; the old ropes weren't too reliable. His mother thought he'd better just get off all together and suggested he go look for eggs in the henhouse. He went off in that direction, but he wasn't about to go in and disturb the chickens.

Gran's house was up off the ground like theirs was at home, with plenty of space to crawl under. He got down on his hands and knees and went in. He liked being in such cool dim places the sun never got to.

Even though there were spider webs and a few dirt dauber nests, he always felt snug and safe there, but at the same time it was secret and strange. The smell from the wood above his head was different from the inside of the house. At home he sometimes spent the whole afternoon under there building houses out of the loose bricks left over from the foundation or digging holes in the smooth dirt to shoot marbles. Now and then he would listen to people talk when they didn't know he could hear, the sounds muffled but coming through the floor clear enough to make out if you found just the right spot.

He edged on up toward where the front porch was and heard his mother's voice. "I'm just at my wit's end, Mama. I can't even try for a job clerking down at the dry goods store until after the baby comes — if I make it through the next three months and don't lose this one. I have got to have some way to put bread on the table for us. It looks like I can't count on Joe and I certainly can't keep taking from you."

"You know what's mine is yours, daughter. We'll manage." He could hear Gran's chair rocking smoothly back and forth. It was easy to imagine how she looked — as if she could handle anything now that Mama sounded like she'd given up on his daddy.

"The little that Papa left is barely enough for you to squeeze by on, even with your dratted boarders." That was the kind of thing he'd never hear from Mama if she had any idea he was listening.

"You and the boy and the new little one are welcome. You can't doubt that. The Lord provides for those who trust Him."

"You've said that and said that, Mama!" There was a bang right over John's head that must have been her foot stomping on the floor. "I'm just not up to sitting back and trusting anymore." Then came the sound of steps walking back and forth. "You know something, Mama? I was lying in there a good part of the night trying to figure it all out and I was about ready to just get up and go walk down the railroad track — simply keep right on walking until I ran smack into a train!"

It was hard to believe that was his mama talking. He imagined her in her long white nightgown, walking in a straight line right toward a locomotive. In his mind he made the locomotive stop in time. His grandmother's voice was shrill.

"I won't hear of that sort of thing in my house! That's the devil's talk!"

"See, Mama? It really is your house. Always will be. But don't worry. I recalled that the train doesn't even come down this little spur but twice a week. I'd likely give out before one showed up."

"I know you don't mean that sinful kind of talk, Eva. I'm not taking it to heart. That's your pain and trouble making you speak that way." Then, "Why look at you! You are indeed in pain, aren't you, child?" There was a sharp moaning cry from one of them. "Eva! What is it?"

A clattering crash came and dribbling sound that

must have been the peas scattering over the porch.

"Oh, God, Mama."

It felt like the locomotive had got going again, was coming closer and this time he couldn't stop it. He slapped his hands over his ears and lay flat on the ground, but he could still hear Gran call "Bella!" and heavy steps running through the house. Mama was losing the baby. He was sure of it. It had happened twice before and there was always a lot of crying and bleeding. He didn't want to see any more blood. He hated it.

He wiggled out of his hiding place and ran toward the henhouse. The mother hen was pecking about nearby, but he kicked at her and ran on in. A cackling chicken fluttered off of her nest, and he took her still warm egg and sat down in the tall weeds behind the henhouse, letting the sun flood into his upturned face, watching the patterns it made on his closed eyelids, trying not to think about anything. But the memory came over him of hiding under the house when Spud got kicked, how he'd run away then, too. There was a hollow feeling in his stomach and he decided that he was fiercely hungry.

It came to him that if he wanted to he could poke a hole in the egg and suck out the insides. Weasels did that. He remembered back to after Spud was killed, when he'd got the dumb notion that his whole family might be going to die, one right after the other. He'd stolen a sack of peanuts out of the pantry and hidden it in a corner of the hayloft so he'd know where to find something to eat if everybody died off and left him. Later on, he started thinking he was the one going to die next. He hadn't, of course. Wasn't going to until he was old as Uncle Oscar and good and ready. It seemed to him he'd lived a very long time already. Forever. He couldn't imagine a time when there wasn't any him.

He wondered if the baby that wasn't going to get born in the regular way would go on back up to Heaven and wait for another chance. Maybe end up in some other family. Maybe God heard all that wicked talk from Mama and changed His mind about letting her have the baby.

John looked around for a sharp twig to poke the egg with. He'd had raw eggs before. Once, when he was getting over malaria fever, he was so skinny and weak that his mama used to make him what he called "egg in a glass," beaten up fizzy with sugar and vanilla flavoring. He broke a long thorn off a bramble bush, made an opening at both ends, and sucked hard on it. Without the sugar and vanilla it tasted awful, like he was drinking something alive. He made himself suck and swallow until the shell was empty and then chewed on a handful of sour grass to get rid of the taste.

He lay back in the weeds and wondered how long he'd have to stay there before it was over and everything was all right again. The way it had been. Surely it was going to be all right. He just had to wait it out. Then he remembered his daddy's words. Watch out for your mama, he'd said. It makes me feel good knowing you can take ahold, he'd said. This was a pretty sorry way to be watching out for anybody, running off where he couldn't see or hear what was happening.

He got up, brushed himself off, and went toward the house.

6

When his mama was taken sick Bella sent him for the doctor. "I was goin' myself, but I might be more of a help here. You know where he got his office?" He didn't and was uneasy about finding his way around Riley. But his daddy had bragged about how he could take ahold of things and how he was counting on him to look after Mama. Bella gave him directions. "Doc Barrett be right up over Tucker Hardware. How you get there is you go down the road thataway a good piece. You come to a big gray house with what look like a little white fence runnin' around the edge of the roof. Great big house. Belong to Mr. Rip Garfield down at the bank. Got a Confederate flag he flies out the upstairs window. You seen it. That goin' to be on yo' left-hand side."

"I remember," said John. "Then which way?"

"Take a left turn straight on past the hotel and then past the livery and after while you come to Tucker Hardware. Tell Doc Barrett yo' mama bleedin' pretty bad."

There were other people in the waiting room when he got there — a man with a swollen jaw and a stringy, pale woman fanning herself and looking miserable. Maybe it wouldn't be fair to ask the doctor to leave them sitting there and go off to see about his mother. They'd have a right to be mad at him. He wished he'd let Bella come instead like she started to. If he waited his turn it might be too late. He walked over to the closed door and knocked on it hard. The man and woman raised their heads and frowned at him. He was bracing himself to say his speech when the door opened a crack and a red-faced little man with a booming voice said, "Well, yes? What is it? Can't you take a seat and wait? Right over there. You'll get your turn."

He almost backed away to do as he was told, but then he heard himself saying, "It's an emergency, sir. Up at Mrs. John Beaumont's house. She said for you to please come right away." Then he added, mostly for the benefit of the others, so they would see he had the right, "Somebody's dying."

"Who is it, son? What happened?"

"It's my mama. She lost the baby and she's bleeding bad."

"I see. Well, what say you run across to the livery stable and have them bring my buggy 'round. I'll finish up some stitching in here and be downstairs in five minutes."

Wondering if he should have said that about dying, he ran down the stairs, relieved that the doctor had

55

believed him but not quite sure he'd told the truth. He didn't really know what the truth was. The doctor's message was easier to handle, more straight out. He could feel important without having to say all that about what the trouble was. He stopped in front of a couple of men who sat with their chairs tipped back and he didn't even apologize for interrupting them. "Doc Barrett says to bring his buggy 'round. It's an emergency. He says to hurry." That got them going.

While they were hitching up, he looked around for Pluto, but he didn't dare to go back past the stalls. One of the last things his mother had said was that she didn't want him in a livery stable. Suppose she died and those very words turned out to be the last thing she ever did say to him! The thought was so awful that he broke into a run and headed for home.

As he ran along the wire fence next to the stable, a familiar voice called, "Hey, what you see yonder, eyes? Ain't that my friend John Bo? Where you headin' so lickety-split, man?" He jerked to a stop and turned to see a black face grinning at him across the back of a potbellied mule.

"Got to get on back," he wheezed, but glad to stop, glad to see a friendly face to tell his misery to. Somebody in the town who knew him by name. He crooked his fingers into the wire fence and sagged against it. "It's my mama, Pluto." The boy came toward him, leading the mule. "Bella says she's taken real bad. Doctor's on the way."

"Aw, man. Sorry to hear that. What Big Mama say is the matter — woman trouble?"

He nodded. "Baby born way before time. I'm the one came and found Doc Barrett. Ran most of the way." It was all right to feel a little proud of himself. He liked it when Pluto called him "man."

"Well, you take it easy now and catch yo' breath. You done every blessed thing a body can do right now. Yonder goes the buggy. It's gonna be all right." Then, "How you like my ugly ole mule I been prettyin' up?"

It was certainly peculiar-looking, but John didn't want to take any chances on hurting Pluto's feelings. "That sure is some mule, all right."

"I calls him Henry. He Mr. Rip Garfield's coon huntin' mule. I names all my mules I works on. I done roach him myself. That mean brush him good and trim down his mane and his tail, see? I been watching ole Jesse do it, but this here the first time they ever let me have a go at it. Henry, say howdy to my buddy, John Bo."

"Howdy, Henry."

"To tell the honest truth, they don't know I done it. Mostly I'm s'pose to just brush off the mud, and Jesse he s'posed to do the roachin', but that fool nigger be drunk as a skunk back in the corn crib."

John couldn't bring himself to call it a good job. The mane stuck up in little spikes and the tail was nearly bare, so he said, "Henry, you look like what my daddy would call a rat-tail mule. Skinny little tail like that."

"I likes a mule to look thata way. I trimmed him close on purpose."

"What else my daddy would call him is a potty, on account of that big fat belly."

"Yo' papa know a whole lot about mules?"

"Sure he does. He spent pretty near a whole week getting the pick of 'em up in Memphis." He didn't tell the rest of the story. "He's probably the best mule trader in this county."

"Well, now. I speck he liable to say, 'Henry, you ain't nothin' but crow bait!' But Pluto here likes yo' looks fine."

Crow bait, thought John. That means being pretty nearly dead and ready for the buzzards and crows to come get you. His mother wasn't really dying, of course. He'd just said that in the doctor's office. "I can't stand here all day talking to a dumb mule," he said. "I got to get word over to my daddy about my mama. He ought to be here. I better be going." But he wasn't a bit sure what to do. He turned back and asked, "You reckon I could walk it and get there before too late?"

Pluto seemed to know what he was thinking before it was clear in his own head. "Too far, man. Way too far. But looka here. I could easy ride over there. I could get the word to him myself. Onliest thing is I don't rightly know the way. Looks like you gonna have to go along with me. How bout that? We can ride double." He acted as if it were all settled.

"Ride what? We ain't got nothing to ride." He began to edge away. "I better go on and try walking." After all, he had made her a promise.

"You ain't thinkin', man. We got Maud, ain't we? That horse got plenty steam left in her." Pluto was warming up to his idea. "Just lemme run tell Mr. Shumway your grandmama needs to go some place again and I'm s'pose to take her horse back home."

"I don't know," said John. "I don't know if I'd be any good at riding."

"No need to be good at it. All you got to do is sit easy in the saddle. I be on behind handling everything."

"Maybe I better just go on back and find out for sure how my mama is. She might be over it and doing all right by now."

"If she done lost that baby, she be pinin' anyhow. Ain't yo' papa gonna want to know 'bout it and grieve 'longside her?"

That did it. The thought of his mama and daddy back together and being a comfort to each other made up his mind for him. "We can use my grandpapa's saddle. The one in the shed at the house."

"You thinkin' smart now, John Bo. We have to sneak it, else Miz Beaumont gonna say, 'Oh, my! Y'all can't do that! Y'all know that child's mama don't want him on no horse.' Right?"

"Right." Sometimes promises had to be broken to protect someone you loved, the way Gran had said about lying.

"Here I go to tell Mr. Shumway. See that gate yonder goin' out to the little alley back there?"

John nodded.

"I meet you right there in a little bit. Come on, Henry."

But Henry had taken a fancy to some grass he was nibbling around the fence post. Pluto dug his heels into the ground, leaned on the bridle, and sweet-talked him. "Come on, now, and show yo'self off. Those other critters in the stable gonna say, 'Look yonder at Henry. Who done roach him up so fine? Wonder can we get him to do a job on us?'"

Sure enough, Henry started back, but before he went in, he flopped down and rolled in the dust, currying his own hide as if Pluto hadn't done the job to suit him after all.

John walked on around the corner into the alley and waited by the gate. It seemed like a long wait but finally Pluto showed up, leading Henry instead of Maud.

"Maud done throwed a shoe and she liable to be over at the blacksmith's shop all afternoon. Me and you gonna ride ole Henry," said Pluto.

"That's stealing," said John.

"This here's borrowin'. For a good reason why. We got to go get yo' papa, ain't we? This the onliest way. I told Mr. Shumway Henry was all finished up and

I'd take him on home. Mr. Garfield come by earlier and want him spruced up and ready to go coon huntin' tonight. I can have this mule back here to say good evenin' to him by the time he get hisself home from the bank."

"Won't the two of us be too much for Henry?"

"Heck, no. If he can carry Mr. Garfield skitterin' through the woods, a heavyset man like that, he ain't gonna mind us doublin' along on a good road. Let's go fetch the saddle."

They took a short cut Pluto knew, Henry trotting along behind as agreeable as pie. "This gonna work fine," said Pluto. "I been cravin' me a ride in the country."

They tied the mule to a sweet gum tree hidden from view by a stand of crepe myrtle bushes back of Gran's house. Looking through the leaves they could see the doctor's buggy hitched to the post, and for one moment John thought how easy it would be to jump into the buggy and take off. Once you tried "borrowing," it seemed a handy way to do things.

"While you get the saddle out the shed, I better go up to the house and let Big Mama know where we headin'. After we be gone, she can tell Miz Beaumont, else she liable to worry herself into conniption fits 'bout what done become of you downtown. Wait till I gets to the kitchen. Then you light out."

John did as he was told. The saddle was in the corner of the shed covered with old flour sacks. It was too big for him but Gran was saving it for when he finally got old enough to ride and grew into it. He dragged it out, sneezing from the dust he raised, and carried it back to Henry. He didn't even look toward the house, trusting that Pluto would stand on his head or something to keep Gran from seeing him if she happened to come back to the kitchen right then.

He waited, wondering what was going on in the room where his mother was. He pushed away the awful picture that formed in his mind and made up a different one in which his daddy came riding up and rushed into the house. He imagined his mother reaching her arms out and saying, "Oh, Joseph! Thank God you have come. How did you know?" And his daddy would say, "Our brave son rode all the way to get me."

When Pluto came back Bella was with him. "How is she?" he asked, afraid to hear.

"It's in the good Lord's hands, child, but Miss Sally and the doctor is in there helpin' out. Your papa ought to be here for sure, but can't you just tell Pluto how to go? Your mama likely to skin me alive if she find out I let you ride."

"I don't think I could," he said, pulling a clump of clover to offer Henry. He might have tried to tell him, but it was easy to get mixed up describing a pointy tree you had to watch for at one turn or the bunch of sumac at another. And anyway, he liked the idea of his daddy saying, "Our brave son rode all that way."

"How 'bout Jesse?" asked Bella. "Couldn't he go? He been out there once before."

"No'm," said Pluto. "He been drinkin' again."

Pluto was tightening the saddle strap and Henry was munching on the clover.

"Well," said Bella, " I better go get y'all some vittles to take along."

"Can't wait," said Pluto. "Anyhow, I took us a couple of biscuits when I was in there. They in my pocket."

It had been a long time since breakfast, but it wasn't hunger that was making John's stomach funny. He was about to do something he had looked forward to and dreaded — both — most of his life.

Pluto had finished saddling and as usual was admiring his work. "Mighty fine!" He slapped the leather seat. "Now, John Bo, if you kindly put yo' foot in the stirrup and then put yo' bottom right here, we be headin' out."

Bella had to help him. His feet didn't quite reach the stirrups once he was up, but he held tight to the saddle horn and pressed his knees into the mule's fat belly. He was glad Henry was a mule instead of a horse. Horses sometimes reared way up on their hind legs. Then he remembered how Henry had flopped down and rolled in the dust, and he wondered if he would have time to jump free if the mule took it into his head to try that again.

Pluto mounted and sat astride Henry's bare back, reaching around John to take the reins. Making a clicky sucking noise and kicking his heels, he said, "Here we go like a streak of lightnin'! Get up, mule!"

But Henry stood stock still, chewing on another mouthful of clover he had helped himself to.

Bella broke a little branch off the tree and gave it to John, but to his relief Henry decided to go before he had to hit him with it.

"For the Lord's sake, y'all be careful," said Bella. Then, "Mr. Garfield say you could use his mule?"

"Yessum. He don't mind," Pluto called back.

John wondered if it was very bad luck to start off with a lie like that.

7

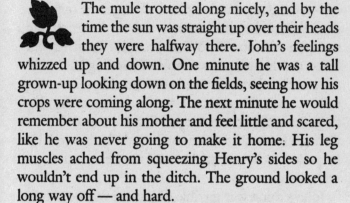 The mule trotted along nicely, and by the time the sun was straight up over their heads they were halfway there. John's feelings whizzed up and down. One minute he was a tall grown-up looking down on the fields, seeing how his crops were coming along. The next minute he would remember about his mother and feel little and scared, like he was never going to make it home. His leg muscles ached from squeezing Henry's sides so he wouldn't end up in the ditch. The ground looked a long way off — and hard.

He wondered whether Pluto had ever been thrown off a horse or mule. If he had, how could he keep on liking to ride as much as he did? Pluto had said riding was more fun than eating — except for ice cream. He'd had some of that once. They were getting close to the iron bridge now. John started to pretend he was Bentley, halfway home from school, thinking he was going to get there, not having the slightest notion what was about to happen. Bentley had been in a saddle the right size for him so that his feet were in the stirrups to steady him, and still . . .

"I think we ought to stop for a little while," John said. "I got to rest my legs."

"It's my sittin' bones I got to rest, and Henry bound to have drinkin' some water on his mind. See how his ears perk up? He can smell that creek yonder."

They slid off and led the mule down through the willow trees on the bank. While he drank they stretched out on the damp sand under the bridge, the only spot shaded from the noonday sun, and ate the crumbling, sat-upon biscuits Pluto had brought. John remembered that he had put a couple of winding balls in his shirt pocket that morning before breakfast, intending to have something to look forward to, and then had forgotten about them with all that happened. It went through his head to save them both for himself, but he pulled them out, sticky from the heat, and shared with Pluto.

John's thirst was terrible, but there was no way he was going to drink creek water the way Pluto did, wading in and cupping it in his hands. Pluto didn't seem to be bothered by the thought of yellow fever germs or all the other awful possibilities that were on John's mind a lot. Maybe he never had bad things happen to him the way John had. That would make a difference.

"Right here's where my brother got killed," he told him.

"Is that a fact? This the place it happened? It's a pretty place, but that don't make it no easier."

John didn't know whether he meant easier for Bentley or easier for him. "Up there by the railing's where they found him. It was some convicts working on contract over at the Dunellen Plantation that came along and brought him home. I saw the trusty with his gun and the first thing I thought was he had shot him."

Pluto had sat straight up and looked at John in a peculiar way. "Man! Coulda been my brother Cephus was one of 'em what brought him to y'all. He was workin' on the chain gang long about then."

"You mean you had a brother at Parchman?" That was hard to believe. Parchman was the state prison where the men who had done bad things wore black-and-white striped suits and worked either in the cotton fields there or at some of the wealthy plantations that could afford to hire extra help at the busy seasons. There'd be a trusty holding a gun on them while they worked and sometimes they were chained together by the ankle so nobody could run away. "You had a brother old enough to be in the penitentiary? How old was he?"

"Cephus be 'bout fourteen when he went in, as I recall. They said he stole something that cost a heap of money from a white lady."

"What kind of a thing was it?"

Pluto pushed his heel back and forth in the sand

67

for a moment before he answered. "A little ole red-eyed owl. You b'lieve that?"

"I never heard of any kind of an owl with red eyes."

"This here was made out of pure gold, she say. Worth 'bout a jillion dollars. S'pose to sit on a lady's bosom with a little watch dangling down from the claws. Got two what you call ruby stones stuck in where the eyes belongs. She swear and declare Cephus done stole it."

"How long was he in for?"

"Judge called for ten years but what it turned out to be was just a few months. The trusty told everybody he was trying to get away and he had to shoot him."

"Shoot him dead, you mean?"

"That's right. It ain't for sure he was even trying to run off. You know trusties gets a pardon whenever they shoots somebody they *says* is trying to escape."

"That's terrible! Somebody ought to do something about it."

Pluto gave a laugh that wasn't a bit funny. "Who? Who you think that gonna be?"

John wished his grandpapa was still living so he could write a piece in the paper about it. It wasn't fair, and he could say so. But he knew there wasn't any point in talking about something that couldn't happen. After a while he just said, "Both of us had the same kind of bad thing happen to us. We both lost a big brother."

"Somebody told me not long ago the lady found that ole owl, after all." Pluto jumped to his feet. "We done had our time out. Got to get movin', man!'"

Getting Henry back up on the road wasn't easy. John tugged at the bridle and Pluto stood out of reach of Henry's hind legs, giving him whacks with a good long switch. After they were up, Pluto seemed to know John wouldn't want to get on the mule again until they'd crossed the bridge, so they walked Henry to the other side. Pluto boosted John up and then swung into place behind him.

After they had ridden for a while without saying anything, John asked, "Did your mama cry a lot, when that happened to your brother, I mean?"

"Mostly she done her cryin' when they put him in. Wailin' in the night like she could tell what was gonna happen. That's how come she beg Big Mama to come take me off to Riley when I got into a little bit of trouble myself. 'O, sweet Jesus, don't let 'em take another of my chillun to Parchman,' she'd say. It was nothin' much, what I done, but it suit me fine to come up here and not have to put up with all that cryin' and carryin' on."

John wanted to ask what he'd done, but he was sure Pluto would tell him straight out if he wanted him to know.

"They wouldn't put anybody your age in the penitentiary."

"My age be just turned twelve, goin' on thirteen. I got a good part of my growth. They might. We heard tell of a child ten years old put in one time. But I'd figure me a way out, and I'd live to tell about it.

69

No way they gonna get ole Pluto. They don't scare me none."

"I think they'd scare me a lot. But I'm not anywhere near the scaredy cat I was back when Bentley and Spud got killed. I got this real dumb idea that all the men in the whole world were going to die. You know how I got such a crazy idea?"

"Naw, how?"

"I was in church one time, right after Spud's funeral. I guess it was a few weeks later, and the choir was singing, mostly ladies. When I heard them sing a part that goes 'World without end, amen,' what I thought they were saying was 'World without men. Ah, men!' — like pretty soon there wouldn't be anything left in the world but just women. I was real little, but I went on thinking that for a while. Pretty funny, huh?" He never had told anybody about that before.

"You musta been a scared little bugger."

"I had the notion my daddy would be the next one to go, or maybe me. That was sure dumb, all right."

"Naw, you was just too little to know the straight of it."

Suddenly Henry, being a hunting mule and not used to long stretches on the road without any shade, took a liking to a stand of trees off to the right, and, in spite of all Pluto's tugging at the reins and all his sweet-talking, made his way into the woods and stood there swishing his skinny tail at the mosquitoes. He wasn't going to leave until he was good and ready.

"Henry, you tryin' to get me in trouble? Yo' good friend Pluto? You stay in this patch of shade all afternoon, I'm the one gonna be crow bait."

But the idea of trouble didn't really seem to bother him much. When John finally said, "You're stubborn as a mule, Henry," Pluto doubled over with laughing and nearly knocked them both off. It seemed like the laughing and yelling were the signal Henry had been waiting for to be good and ready. He took off, got back on the road, and went faster than ever, as if he wanted to make up for lost time.

When they turned in at the gate, John called a loud hello, wanting his daddy to get a look at him on the mule. But the only answer was from Lucy, who came out from her cool spot under the house, baying a welcome and thrashing her tail with pleasure. They rode on into the barn and found the wagon and mules gone. It had never occurred to John that his daddy might not be at home when they got there, and he couldn't think what to do next.

But one thing they had to do was get off, tie up Henry, and get him a handful of hay. A long cool drink of pump water was for sure the next thing after that. Pluto was too busy looking around the yard and getting acquainted with Lucy to settle down and put his mind to what they ought to do, so John went into the empty house and checked out each room. Everything was so still and lonesome that he thought he might start to cry, but he found a plate of cold string beans and onions in the kitchen and remembered how

71

hungry he was. He took two forks and carried the plate out to the back porch.

While he and Pluto sat on the steps eating, they saw Haze coming in from the cornfield where he had been chopping weeds. Pluto put down his fork and ran toward him, flapping his long arms and calling, "Hey, Uncle Haze! Kinfolks done come! I betcha you don't even know me!"

"For the Lord's sakes, if it don't be Plutie, growed up to be man-size almost! I declare — just look at you!" said Haze, slapping Pluto's back and hugging him. They were making over one another so much that John felt it was too bad to have to break into all that celebration with bad news.

"Haze, we come to get daddy. Where is he? Mama's bad off — lost the baby, I'm pretty sure — and he needs to get over there."

"Aw, don't tell me that!" said Haze. "Miss Eva got to go through all that sorrow and misery again? That's a shame. Mister Joe gonna want to be there, but he done gone to Crawford to look for work on the big new church they building over there. Took the mules and wagon so's to carry along a heap of tomatoes and cushaws to sell in town. Tell me, how y'all get here?"

"Rode double on a mule. He's tied up in the barn."

"I'm gonna have to go after yo' papa. I know the place they doing the building. I can ride the mule y'all come on."

For a moment John was relieved that Haze was

taking over. Then it dawned on him what would happen. Pluto wasn't going to get Henry back to Mr. Garfield in time and would be in terrible trouble. He would end up being crow bait, like he said. But if they waited until his daddy came back it might be sundown. He could tell by the look on Pluto's face that he was turning it all over in his mind. Haze was already heading for the barn.

"We got to tell him, Pluto. My daddy'll just have to wait until morning. You got to take that mule back."

"I reckon," said Pluto, looking disappointed that it wasn't going to turn out the way he'd planned it. "Wait, Uncle Haze, I got to tell you sumpin' 'bout that mule," he called, and both boys ran to where Haze was adjusting the stirrups.

"What you got to tell me, Plutie?"

"Well, you see, what happened is . . . I mean, what I got to explain to you is . . . I done took . . ." Pluto gave a little pretend cough and said politely, "Excuse me." Then he shrugged his shoulders. "What I mean to say is, I done took care of that mule myself and what you have to do when he turn stubborn is you have to sweet-talk him."

Haze laughed and got on Henry. "You think I don't know mules, boy? What's the matter with you? You stay 'round here, I'll learn you aplenty 'bout mules." He grinned at Pluto. "Go yonder and tell yo' Aunt Dancie she having company for supper. Tell her to fix you up a bed, too. I be back fo' dark." Then, "Don't you fret, Little John. I'm gonna find yo' papa. It's gonna be all right. Get up here, mule."

"Look at that Henry take off!" said Pluto. "Fast as greased lightning!"

"Why'd you let him go?" asked John, wondering if he should have been the one to stop him. "What's gonna happen to you now?"

"Aw, not too much. A lickin' or two prob'ly. But I likes things to work out how we planned. Anyhow, I got to get acquainted with my kinfolks, ain't I? Come on here. I wants to go meet my Aunt Dancie."

8

 Dancie had been sewing when they knocked on the door, and the bed was covered with cut-out pieces of material. Pluto introduced himself.

"Aunt Dancie, I ain't had the pleasure of meetin' you before, but I be Elmore and Irene's boy, Pluto."

Dancie didn't do any of the squealing and hugging Haze did, but you could tell she was glad to see him. She raised her chin and turned her head to look at him sideways for a good long while, as if she was taking in every single thing about him. Then she reached out her hand for him to shake and offered her cheek for him to kiss, and only then gave him a smile and asked what he was doing there. Pluto told her why they had come and that they would be spending the night.

"We be proud to have you, son," said Dancie, sounding like she really meant it. John wondered if he was going to have to sleep up in the house all by himself. Dancie hadn't said anything about being proud to have him.

"You go show Pluto around, Little John," she said. "I got to get this here dress finished. Lady from Riley comin' out to pick it up tomorrow."

So John and Lucy and Pluto walked around the place that was so much smaller now than it used to be, but they checked out the garden and the barn and John even took him down past the cornfield and down the road to the little shack that served as the Black Creek school. It was boarded up for summer, but they sat down in the play yard and had a lesson in reading. Pluto took a stick and wrote PLUTO in the dirt.

"What's the rest of your name? Is there some more to it?" John hadn't thought much about the fact that you never heard anything but colored people's first names — that was just how it was — like you almost never knew the last names of people in the Bible.

"My family name be Johnson," said Pluto, "same as Big Mama and Uncle Haze and Aunt Dancie. We all go by Johnson. But what I can write good is just the Pluto part."

"Here's how you make Johnson. More than half of it's my name. We got some of the same name." And he wrote the letters out for him.

"Yeah! I remember now. I seen that before. And you know how come I never took to learnin' it? Didn't seem like it make no sense. See, this here letter O in Pluto sound exactly like O. Plut-o. Then O come along here two times in Johnson; don't sound nothin' like O."

"That's what's hard about reading, all right. There's more than one way to say all the letters. The Beau part of my middle name sounds like O when there ain't an O in it a-tall. Lots of it doesn't make good sense. But don't worry, I'll show you. You'll get it after a while, but right now you just learn Johnson, 'cause then you'll be able to read and write my name, too. Try it."

Before they left the schoolyard, Pluto had written PLUTO JOHNSON CAN WRITE GOOD, written it big, and written it little over all the bare ground there was. He had complained that it didn't make any sense for the two O's stuck right together in "good" not to sound a bit like any of the other ones, but he kept at it anyhow until he did a whole sentence without looking at the last one he'd written. They went back to the house, both of them feeling pretty smart by that time.

John found the old slate Bentley used with him and let Pluto practice on that, showing him how to hold the chalk just right. It was harder than simply grabbing on to a stick, and it was very hard to write little enough to get it all on the slate, but when Pluto decided to learn something there was no stopping him. He had made up his mind to surprise Haze and Dancie that evening, and he kept rubbing the slate clean with his shirt sleeve and starting over.

John was getting bored with that one sentence, and since he was bored, he went back to worrying about his mama.

"Colored people are supposed to be able to feel things in their bones, aren't they? What do you think, Plutie?" He liked the name Haze and Dancie used and decided he'd use it from now on. "Do you think Haze has found my daddy by now? What do you feel in your bones?"

Pluto stopped writing, pressed his lips together, and shut his eyes for a moment. Then he got up and went outside. He drew a straight line on the ground and stood with one foot on either side of it. Taking out his pocketknife, he opened it, held it out shoulder high above the line, and let it go. It quivered in the ground to the right of the line.

"Got nothin' to worry 'bout. Answer be yes. He done found him all right."

Gran would call it a silly superstition, but it made John feel a lot better.

"Something else you want to know 'bout?"

He was afraid to ask if his mama was all right and just got Pluto to show him how he flipped his wrist when he played mumbley peg. When they finally heard the rumble of the wagon they ran down the narrow dirt road, but Haze was the only person riding in it.

John's daddy had gone on to Riley on the mule. He was probably almost there by the time Haze drove the wagon in. He wouldn't be thinking who Henry belonged to, of course. Just thinking about getting there fast and worrying over Mama. Since Mr. Garfield was planning on going hunting he'd yell bloody murder about Henry not being there. No telling what he and Mr. Shumway would do to Pluto.

But Pluto wasn't acting like he was worried a bit. His face was all lit up with Haze and Dancie making over him so much. They ate a supper of turnip greens and cornbread and fried green tomatoes, and Dancie opened up her last jar of the pears she'd put up last fall. They ate on a wobbly table out on the porch in case there might be a breeze, but the mosquitoes were so fierce that Haze had to light the smudge pot in the yard so they wouldn't be eaten up. Everybody's eyes stung from the smoke, and they all kept wiping tears even while they were giggling over the crazy things Pluto would tell. There was likely more to eat at Gran's house, but John was glad to be here instead, now that he knew his daddy was taking care of things with Mama.

After a while, before it got too dark to see, Pluto got up from the table. Earlier on, he had swept the ground bare in front of the steps and got himself a good stick that he laid ready at the edge of the porch. Now he announced, "Y'all watch. I got something to show you." Biting on his lip to help him remember, he wrote his sentence in the dirt, but he got the *g* and *d* backward in "good." John had taught him to make four *o*'s and put a little stick by the first and last one, but he got them going the wrong way, and it came out "doog."

Haze acted the way Pluto and John had expected — tickled that his nephew was so smart. "Looka here! I declare, Plutie done learnt writin'. Dancie, what you think of that? I been tellin' you, folks in my family got more sense than most. What's it say, Plutie?"

"Say 'Pluto Johnson can write good.' "

"How come you know how to do that?"

"I already knowed the Pluto part. My buddy John Bo learnt me the rest. This part here is where it says 'Johnson.' That's y'all's names, too. Want me to help you learn how to write it?"

"What for?" Dancie said, frowning. "What earthly good you think it's gonna do you or us to make fancy scratches in the dirt?"

"What ail you, Dancie?" asked Haze. "You know it be a fine thing to know writin'."

"Ain't gonna be one bit of help to him to scratch his name in dirt. When some little white boy ain't got nothin' better to do one day, to fill up the time he teach you a cute little trick like that. Like 'Come here, Lucy. I'm gonna teach you to roll over. Come here, Plutie, I'm gonna teach you yo' name.' "

"Aw, Dancie! It ain't like that a-tall. Little John done taught Plutie 'cause Plutie got a wish to know. Ain't that right, y'all?"

John didn't know what to say. He'd always had the notion that Dancie didn't much like him, and now here it was coming out. It was Pluto who answered, "I can learn him lots of stuff, too, Aunt Dancie. He don't know ridin' or mumbley peg — or roachin' mules."

"Or milkin'," said Haze.

"It don't go just one way," said Pluto.

"What I mean is," Dancie started and stopped. She took a deep breath, putting her elbows on the table, her two wrists pressed against her forehead, and her long fingers working. "It's wrong to say Plutie can write. He can't write. Writin' and readin' and learnin' enough to do any kind of good take a real school, take plenty time off to go to it and work at it. How in the name of God is Plutie goin' to learn all he need to know for things to be any better for him? Even if he give it some kind of try, they start sayin' this nigger don't know his place. He liable to end up like his brother."

Haze reached out and rubbed her back. "What done set you off so, darlin'? Plutie was just lookin' to please you, like he brung you a present, and here you jump all over it."

Dancie gave a sigh and smiled a little crooked smile at Haze. "It's just that what he done wrote says 'Pluto Johnson can write doog.' You don't know that, Haze, and that don't matter. I do know it, and that don't matter, either."

"You can read, Dancie!" John said. "I didn't know that."

"Whole lot you don't know 'bout me, Little John," she said, "and likely never will."

For a minute it was so quiet you could hear the mules snuffling in the barn. Then Pluto spoke. "We had us a real good time. Me and John Bo is friends, Aunt Dancie."

"Yeah, I guess. For a little while yet, 'til you both gets to be mens and you be sayin', 'Yes, sir, Mister John, what can I do for you, Mister John, sir?'"

But right then she leaned over and spooned some more of the pears onto Pluto's plate and then onto John's. "Finish these up, honey," she said right to him. He could hardly believe he had heard right — her calling him honey instead of Little John, the name he'd been wishing for a long time they'd stop using. "Honey" was friendly all right, but it wasn't a name for a person you'd expect to take ahold of things. No more than Little John was.

"I'm sorry I blew up like that, Haze," she said. "It ain't the child's fault, I guess. Leastways, not yet. Go on and eat yo' pears, Little John."

It was as if Pluto could see right inside his head.

"I don't think y'all ought to call him Little John, Aunt Dancie. It ain't good for him to be called by a baby name like that."

"I sho ain't ready to call him no Mister John. And John all by itself be a little choppy name. I reckon I could do with callin' the name you use, Plutie. You like to be called by that?" she asked John.

He nodded.

"Well, then, lemme ask you somethin' else, John Bo. You like me to make you a pallet here on the porch to sleep on tonight, 'longside Plutie?"

"Yessum," he said, and it felt right to say it that way, no matter what anybody thought. "I'll go on up to the house and bring back some pillows and stuff."

9

The smudge pot went out sometime in the middle of the night and a mosquito woke John up whining around his ear. His legs ached and the porch floor felt hard through the doubled-up quilt he was lying on. He had fallen asleep earlier, even before he got to the end of his prayers. Right after he had asked God to look after his mama and not to let Pluto get into trouble over Henry, it was like he sank down into a thick soft black pillow. Now here he was, stiff and wide awake, watching a lopsided moon low on the horizon, listening to Pluto breathing nearby.

He started to think about all that had happened the day before. Finding the doctor, riding a mule, being in on taking a mule that didn't belong to him, if you were of a mind to look at it that way. Making an honest-to-goodness friend. He whispered it very softly to himself. "I have me a friend now."

He wished he could be more like Pluto, able to get by no matter what happened, sure he could handle anything that came along one way or another. He wished he could be that way, but having a friend like that was the next best thing. Then he remembered what Dancie had said. The time was going to come when they couldn't be friends any longer. Just because Pluto was colored and he was white. It was crazy. Why would it have to be any different just because they got bigger? And at the same time he knew it was going to be. Colored people and white people didn't do things the same. Well, at least they did them in different places — different churches, different schools, if there were any colored schools around.

He'd never given it much thought that colored children weren't expected to go to school much, that there weren't any in the dumpy little school he went to at Black Creek, and as far as he knew there weren't any schools just for them hereabouts. Gran was always talking about how she expected him to get a whole lot of learning and grow up to be important, maybe run a newspaper like Grandpapa had. Yet here he was holding back from going to a real school in Riley to learn all the stuff he'd need to know, worrying over not being smart enough, scared of not knowing anybody. He could just imagine how Pluto would take to it if he had half a chance.

Just as he was thinking that, the smooth sound of Pluto's breathing turned peculiar. There were little whimpers and moans and some mumbled words. He was having a bad dream. Suddenly he cried out, "Naw, sir, don't! Don't now!" John crawled over and shook him by the shoulder. "Lemme go!" he cried.

85

"Hush up, Plutie. It's all right."

In the moonlight, tears sparkled on Pluto's dark cheeks as he sat up and heaved his breath in and out, his shoulders hunched. John kept on telling him it was all right, but all wrong was what it seemed. Pluto scared like that. Pluto who was never scared of anything.

"They brung the hounds. Where they at?" he asked in a hoarse whisper, still confused and shaking.

"Listen, Plutie. You're right here on the porch at Haze and Dancie's. Ain't nothing after you. This is me, John Bo, your good buddy. Remember?"

Pluto looked at him and finally seemed to come awake.

"Have mercy! How you feelin', John Bo?"

"You were having a real bad dream, a nightmare."

"Aw-w, well. Yeah. I reckon I was."

"What was it? What were you dreaming about?"

"Aw, it wasn't much of nothin'. Was I hollerin'?" Pluto seemed kind of ashamed that John might have seen him acting scared.

"Something awful was after you, Plutie. But it's all right. It was just an ole dream. What was it about?"

"Bloodhounds was coming after me, I think it was. Something like that. Ain't dreams crazy? Wonder what put such a thing in my head."

"Maybe worrying over Mr. Garfield and Henry did it."

"Shoot, no. I wouldn't be surprised it was them green tomatoes Aunt Dancie give us for supper. I
86

don't take much to green tomatoes. Sorry I done mess up yo' good night's sleep, man, wakin' you up thata way."

Pluto lay down and seemed to go on back to sleep. John lay slapping at mosquitoes for a long time, remembering how he had sometimes heard the baying of bloodhounds in the night, tracking down somebody who'd run off from the chain gang. He kept turning over in his mind the idea that a person could be pretty scared on the inside and go right on acting brave. But then another thought started to bother him. Pluto talked about getting a couple of lickings for the business about the mule, but both of them seemed to take it for granted that nobody would give John such a licking. After all, he'd been in on the "borrowing," hadn't he? Did it make so much difference, him being white and Pluto being colored that Pluto was expected to take all the blame?

John had thought Haze would drive him and Pluto back to Riley the next day, but Dancie said he had work that needed tending to and they ought to just wait and drive back with the lady who was coming out to pick up the clothes. Haze said maybe Mr. Joe would be back by then and tell that everything was fine.

"Anyhow," said Dancie, "I think y'all owe me a blackberry pickin'. Y'all go down yonder and pick me a heap of berries to pay back for eatin' up the last of my pears." It didn't sound like she was being mean.

It was more like she wasn't ready to let go of Pluto just yet, treating him like he was her boy. She handed each of them a pail and said, "Don't y'all come back here 'til you done pick me plenty for a pie."

They ran through the cotton fields, racing each other down separate rows to reach the place where the brambles grew, and then they raced to see whose pail would fill up faster.

"You ain't got a chance," Pluto kept teasing. "You slow as Christmas, man!" It was hard to think this was the same Pluto as the one shaking and whimpering in the middle of the night. Neither one of them had mentioned the bad dream. And they hadn't mentioned all Dancie had said about reading and writing lessons the night before. John decided to bring the subject up as they passed by the schoolhouse on their way back, figuring they had enough for two or three pies, grinning at each other to show their teeth blue with berry juice.

"What kind of a school was it you went to for a while?" John asked.

"It wasn't no real school like that one sittin' yonder," said Pluto. "It was a lady what used to be a slave when she was a little child. Folks what owned her took a shine to her and learnt her how to read and write. She try to pass some of it on. She let chillun come sit around her kitchen table when they ain't got to be out in the field. I reckon Dancie might have learnt thata way. But like she say, it don't hardly seem worth the trouble to most."

"It sure is hard when you first go at it, but it gets to be fun after a while, being able to read stories and all." He wanted Pluto to think it was worth the trouble. He liked watching him catch on to things. Not a bit like trying to teach something to Clem.

Last night after the nightmare, when he'd been so worried about what might happen to Pluto over the mule and the other thing, he tried to make himself feel better by imagining the exact way he'd like everything to be. His mama would be well and would have a little girl baby to fuss over. A girl might last better than boys did. His daddy would have a real good job in town, maybe as a blacksmith, and make enough to buy some mules to trade on the side. Pluto would decide to stay on right here with his kinfolks, learning to read and helping out with the mules. That would suit Haze and Dancie just fine. He'd teach him everything he learned in school, the way Bentley used to do him. John was sure Pluto could learn anything he put his mind to.

"It wouldn't take you long. You could even read about who you were named for. You'd like that, wouldn't you?"

"I druther some kind of learnin' that'd put plenty money in my pocket. Reckon you could teach me a cute little trick like that?" he asked, pulling his face into a silly look, and bringing out in the open all the stuff Dancie had said about a little white boy with nothing better to do than teach dumb useless tricks to a colored one.

89

"I got a dog I can teach tricks to. I thought you wanted to learn. I don't care one way or another." He picked up a chunk of dirt and threw it toward the schoolhouse. "It don't make a speck of difference to me."

"Aw, man. Lucy most too old to learn. You do better on me. Don't pay Dancie no never mind. But the truth is, I be bound to catch on a whole lot quicker if you got book learnin' what's gonna put a heap of money in my pocket."

John thought about all the kind of work he'd ever heard of colored men doing — plowing fields, chopping cotton and picking it, shoveling dirt to build levees, clearing swampland, handling mules — tough, hard work that needed doing, that didn't call for knowing what was in books. But none of those jobs was going to put much money in a person's pocket.

"There's ways to do that without a whole lot of learning, I guess." He was thinking about whoever had taken the money away from his daddy. Probably that person couldn't read a lick. "Anybody can be a low-down crook and steal money. But you never would do that."

"Naw, I reckon. Less I got too hungry. Never can tell what you liable to do if you gets too hungry." They walked on, thinking about that. After a while, Pluto said, "Cephus never did steal no ole red-eyed owl. Wouldn't have made good sense for him to. Where he gonna sell such a thing, please tell me, to

90

get him some money? He sho' ain't gonna be flashin' it on his overalls 'round town lookin' to see what time it is."

"They locked him up in the penitentiary just because the lady said he took it? When they couldn't prove a thing?"

"That's the Lord's truth, man. See, Cephus used to help her 'round the house diggin' her garden, choppin' firewood, such as that. One day she had him upstairs waxing the hall floor, down on his knees, rubbin' the wax on with a rag. When he come to the end of the hall, Cephus kept right on waxing into the next room. In a minute here she come upstairs. Say, 'Boy, what you doin' here in my room? Ain't nobody tole you to come crawling in here where it ain't nobody to keep an eye on you.' She march right over to her bureau and pull out her jewelry box and give a screech cause the red-eyed owl ain't in there. She start to rave and carry on saying he the onliest one there so he bound to stole it. Then she say Cephus up and sass her. I ain't surprised at that. He got a low boilin' point. Used to have, I mean."

John tried to think how it would have felt if that trusty who brought Bentley home really had shot him, the way he thought at first. What if Bentley had been put in the pen because somebody said he'd done a bad thing when he never had.

"Don't you want to go get even with somebody?"

"Lord help me, I already done heave a rock through that lady's fancy parlor window glass. She got this window all different colors she mighty proud of. I pure ruint it. That's what done got me in trouble back home. I took a ravin' myself when I hear that ole owl be roostin' right there in her room all the time. My mama's cousin was helpin' the lady do her spring cleanin' and come upon it down in a box of mending settin' in the back of her closet. Coulda fallen off a dress, I reckon. Maybe. Anyhow, she told Mama 'bout it."

"They know it was you did it?"

"They got a pretty good idea. Nobody seen me do it, but I couldn't leave it alone. I kept goin' back at night and wailin' outside her house like I be Cephus's ghost. Her brother catch me one night and say he gonna have the Klan or the sheriff after me. One or the other. That's when Mama sent me off to stay with Big Mama."

"I wish I was brave enough to go down there and break another window for her." But even as John said it, he knew that if he did, there wouldn't be the same kind of punishment.

"I don't no way feel like I got even. But it don't eat at me like it used to. Sometime I think about what I'm gonna do if I cross the path of the man what shot Cephus."

"What do you reckon you'd do?"

"It come to me to do all kind of mean things. Then I gets to thinkin' 'bout that trusty wantin' to be out of there so bad he could let hisself do a terrible thing like that. 'Member I told you a trusty can go free if he shoot somebody runnin' off? But could be, the trusty didn't b'long in no Parchman any more than Cephus in the first place."

"Somebody ought to make a law so such a rotten thing couldn't happen anymore."

"Yo' book learnin' gonna show us how to do that? I be willin' to give it my number-one best thinkin' if it did."

"Sure! You and me could have us a printing press. I'd write stuff for the newspaper and you could be the printer, run the printing press and take care of it. It takes a whole lot of machinery. You could fix up machinery instead of fixing up mules."

"How 'bout some of the other way round?" Pluto asked. "I write and you fix?"

That was a pretty funny idea. John thought Pluto was joking, but then again, maybe he wasn't. He didn't look like he meant it for a joke.

"You'd have to do a mighty heap of learning to do that, though."

"You, too, man."

John realized his face was turning red. They walked on through the field without saying anything more until a cloud of dust rose up down the road. Somebody was coming.

Pluto looked a little uneasy for a moment before he took both pails of blackberries and headed for the corn patch. "I best take these here berries on over to Aunt Dancie. You go see who's comin'." And he disappeared between the rows of tall corn.

His daddy had gotten a ride back in the buggy with Mrs. Emmaline Plummer, who played the organ at Gran's church. Sure enough, Mama had lost the baby, but his daddy said not to worry — she was going to be all right. John and his daddy sat in the kitchen and talked it all over while Mrs. Plummer was trying on her dress back in Dancie's house. Pluto was nowhere to be seen.

"It was a mighty close call for her, son, and you did right to come riding out here to get me. That showed gumption, managing to do that."

John knew the gumption was mostly Pluto's, but he said thank you, just the same. "I guess she must be pretty upset over losing the baby," he said.

"Absolutely. She wanted it. Needed it. But somehow, in the middle of all the grieving, it seemed like we got back to showing we cared for one another. I don't know if she plans on coming back here any time soon, though."

The old worries came tumbling back. "You going to be able to get work at the big church over in Crawford?"

"I got to get myself back over there to see. That's how come I didn't stay with your mama longer. Tomorrow's Saturday. I got to be sure of some kind of work bright and early Monday."

"What kind of jobs are they hiring for?"

"All they were willing to offer me for sure yesterday was as a carpenter's helper at only fifteen cents an hour. That's pretty sorry pay."

"Don't they have something better you could get?"

"What they call finished carpenters get more, but I hate to tell you how far I am from finished along that line. It's being talked around that they might bring a bunch of brick masons down all the way from Memphis for thirty-five cents an hour. Say they can't find enough able ones hereabouts. That would be more to my liking."

"I bet you could do that all right. Remember how you had to patch up the bricks under our house?"

"That wasn't any kind of fancy work like what they need. But if I had a chance to practice up, I might could handle something like that. They expect you to put in a twelve-hour day. That would turn into pretty good money. I could maybe even put a little something aside then."

"And start back to buying mules one day?"

"That's a thought, son. But of course the church job would mean leaving home long before daylight and getting back past dark."

"Else you could stay over in town somewhere that didn't cost much," John said, and right away wished he hadn't. There were places that sold whiskey in Crawford.

"Well, maybe. But they think it wouldn't take more than six months to finish. I could stick out the going and coming that long, I reckon. It would be hard on your mama, if she was here, though."

Pluto came to the door then, and John realized that he hadn't even thought to ask about what happened

95

with Henry. "This is Bella's grandson, Daddy. Pluto's the one who got us out here."

"We sure appreciate your help, Pluto," he said and shook hands with him just like he was a grown person. It turned out that when John's daddy took the mule back to the livery stable that morning, Mr. Shumway had really exploded. Not only was he mad because Pluto ran off with the mule, he was mad because of the peculiar way Henry looked, after the roaching Pluto had given him.

"I don't know if it would be wise for you to go back to the livery stable, Pluto," John's daddy said, after they had told him the whole story. "Shumway really hit the ceiling when he saw the mule. He said Mr. Garfield would be of a mind to wear you to a frazzle if he ever catches you."

"What you reckon I ought to do, Mr. Greer?" Pluto asked.

"Well, maybe you should go on back home to your mama. In fact, when he asked where you were, I believe I did say you'd probably headed on down there."

"Naw, sir. I don't believe I'd be none too welcome back at Mama's just yet."

John wanted to ask about letting him stay on there, but he wished Pluto would be the one to bring it up. He wasn't even sure Pluto would want to. Suppose they asked him and he just laughed and said, "Man, what you think a smart fellow like me gonna do stuck way out here in the country?"

But then his daddy was saying, "Why don't you lay low around here a couple more days 'til those two gentlemen have a chance to cool down?" Pluto looked like that suited him just fine, but what he said was, "Big Mama gonna be wondering if I run into trouble."

"John can let her know. Son, your mama needs you over there with her right now. It's going to take a while for her to get her strength back, and having you around should ease her mind a little."

"You mean today? This afternoon?" He didn't want to be in town if Pluto was out here.

"I told her I'd send you along with Mrs. Plummer."

"Did she raise a fuss over me riding out here?"

"Just middling. You were safe and sound before she heard anything about it. But now don't you count on her letting you off of that promise." He got up and left the kitchen to go look for Haze.

"Shoot! I wish the baby had happened — had been born right," John told Pluto. "She's gonna say I'm all she's got in this world. I hate it when she says that."

"I guess the good Lord must think you be enough of a handful for anybody to have to put up with." John gave Pluto a poke in the ribs and then chased him out into the back yard where they started a friendly tussling that kept up until Mrs. Plummer was ready to go. As soon as she came out with her new dress on her arm, Pluto whistled to Lucy and headed for the barn.

"Who's that yonder, Dancie?" Mrs. Plummer asked,

nodding toward Pluto. "He's one of yours, is he?"

John was surprised to hear her answer, "Oh, he just some child from down the road come up to play with Mr. Joe's little boy."

Dancie didn't trust any white people. Somehow that made John sure she'd do a good job of looking after Pluto. She might even help him some with his reading if he sweet-talked her the way he did mules. He sure wished he didn't have to leave. He wished they'd had a chance to talk some more about what they could do when they grew up.

His daddy gave him a bundle of stuff to take with him, a few green onions and some bell peppers and one of the cushaws Gran had bragged on. Then he made John run wash his face and hands at the pump before he climbed into the buggy waiting out front with Mrs. Plummer settling herself inside. Pluto called from the barn, "John Bo! I done thought up a name for that paper, man. We could call it the *Doog News*. How you like that?"

"You're plum crazy!" John answered, feeling good that Pluto was still thinking about what he'd said, and feeling good that they were friends.

Mrs. Emmaline Plummer was a well-to-do lady with two chins, who took up more than her half of the buggy seat. He'd heard Gran say she'd gone away to a college up North and used the English language so beautifully that it put the rest of the folks roundabout to shame. John wondered what on earth they'd talk about all the way back, as he sat with the vegetables

98

at his feet and her new dress on his lap, trying to keep tissue paper tucked around it so the dust wouldn't get all over it.

"I was most distressed to learn of your mother's suffering a miscarriage," she said, using a word John hadn't heard before but which he figured meant lost the baby. "Take her my sincere condolences, won't you?"

Then she started talking about what a remarkable seamstress Dancie was. "It is positively astonishing how one can show that woman a picture from the rotogravure and have her produce a quite satisfactory garment without resorting to a pattern of any sort." She gave a tinkly little laugh and touched her handkerchief to her forehead. "I only wish our Maker had thought fit to bestow such a talent on one of the less competent white women in town who call themselves seamstresses. 'Twould be ever so much more convenient."

John wondered if she really talked like that all the time, wondered if that was how people sounded after they got a really good education. He was also glad Dancie hadn't let her know who Pluto was. He wasn't sure why.

She began to tell him about her little girl, Daisy, who was about his same age. "My Daisy's an inveterate reader. There are times when I simply have to forbid the child to spend any more time absorbed in her books and send her out for some wholesome diversion."

When she asked him if he enjoyed reading and what his favorite book was, he told her it was *Robin Hood*, but then was embarrassed because he couldn't remember the name of the person who wrote it.

"Come now! You mustn't be careless with such details if you're going to grow up to be a professional man," she said, "and I know your dear grandmother has high hopes for your future."

He could just imagine the sort of thing Gran had told her. She liked to brag to people about how smart he was, but now Mrs. Plummer was finding out the truth about him, that he was pretty ordinary and had a hard time getting the straight of what a person with a good education was talking about.

"Daisy is well on her way to becoming a scholar. But she, too, has certain weaknesses. She isn't thoroughly proficient in spelling, I have to admit. For example, she was confounded in the spring spelling bee over a simple word like *hippopotamus*. Lengthy but certainly simple. Can you imagine?" The tinkly little laugh again. "I have no doubt you could have spelled it, John, could you not?"

He couldn't. She kept on talking about what Daisy could and couldn't do until he was sure he never wanted to go to school after he got finished with Black Creek. He certainly never wanted to go to Riley. He could imagine every child his age spelling *hippopotamus* and multiplying fractions and treating him the way everybody treated Clem — like he was kind of pathetic. Now Mrs. Plummer was asking about his school.

"There are ten of us in all go there. Nobody's the same age as anybody else."

"And have you a qualified teacher?"

"Ma'am?"

"A college-trained person? Has she a degree in education?"

He said yes, but he was pretty sure Miss Polk never went to college. She certainly didn't talk anything like Mrs. Plummer and lots of times had to look up the answers in the back of the arithmetic book herself.

"Well, I know your grandmother is counting on your attending a more rigorous school here in Riley before long, and I have no doubt you'll make splendid headway then."

He didn't want to go. A rigorous school sounded awful. By the time they reached Gran's house, he'd thought up several different things to say to persuade his mama to go back home so he could keep on at Black Creek, where they didn't know he wasn't very smart.

10

Before John went in to see his mama, Gran took him into her room and gave him a talking-to. First she praised the Lord for His manifold blessings. Mama was going to be all right. Then she asked him to join her in a little word of prayer. She went on for a good while about how we down here below couldn't know what was best for the little baby that didn't get to live, because God moves in mysterious ways. John had always known that was the truth. Sometimes he tried to think what he would do if he was God and could make anything happen or not happen just because he wanted it that way. He was pretty sure he could do a better job of managing the world. When he was little he didn't know any better than to say such a thing out loud, and Gran told him he was getting close to the sin of blasphemy. She'd made it sound like a terrible place to be. "Our ways are not His ways," she had said and made him learn by heart some verses in the Bible that said so. Now and then he wondered if a lot of bad things happened because he'd thought so many wicked thoughts. While he had his eyes shut, without saying it out loud, he asked God to forgive him for sometimes thinking He didn't know what He was doing. Then he added on one more prayer that his mama would hurry up and go on back home and finish up getting well there.

After the praying was over, Gran said what he knew she was bound to say. "Now, John Beaumont, you're the one who'll have to make it up to her for losing the baby. Be a good boy and make her proud of you. Make her happy again. You can do it."

No, he couldn't. He didn't know how. It felt like way too much for him to manage. Why should it all be up to him, anyway?

"Daddy's coming over on Sunday," he said.

"Well," she said. "Of course." And she acted like he had changed the subject.

When he finally went in to see his mama she was lying in bed looking a lot different from how he remembered her the morning before. Her stomach was flat now. There were brown circles under her eyes, and she was too worn out to even hug him a good tight hug. She just touched his face and gave a little sad smile.

All of a sudden he wished he could turn himself into a tiny new baby she could cuddle up and lay her cheek against the way she used to do with Spud. That would make her happy. She wouldn't look so lonesome lying there, and nobody would expect him to do anything except eat and be little and cute. Nobody would expect him to go to a hard school where he didn't know anybody, to get a good education so he'd make her proud.

"You feel all right?" he asked. He wished he'd brought her something, some flowers from home, maybe. She sighed and nodded. "Looks like you aren't going to get that little baby sister we'd hoped for," she said, her hand falling limp on the sheet.

"No'm. Daddy told me. I'm sorry."

"Doctor Barrett says I ought to quit trying." She turned away and looked out of the window. He wanted her to say it didn't really matter. He wanted her to say that just as long as he and his daddy were around it would be a good solid family. They'd be plenty for each other.

"I reckon maybe the good Lord just decided I'd be enough of a trouble for anybody to have to put up with." He thought she might think that was funny. Pluto had thought so. But instead she gave a little gasp and took hold of his arm, tight.

"Don't talk that way! You've never been a trouble to me. You've been my salvation, child. You know you have." She seemed to get her strength back all of a sudden and raised herself up from the pillow. "You are so precious to me. You mustn't take any more chances the way you did yesterday. If anything were to happen to you . . ." She shook her head and lay back down. She didn't say the words, but what she meant was it would kill her. Put her in her grave. He was her salvation.

"You'd still have Daddy, wouldn't you?" He had to know about that.

She gave him a funny look and after a long moment she nodded. "I would. I'd still have your daddy, John. But listen now, I mean it. I don't want to hear of you doing any kind of riding again before next year. Understand?"

After he had promised and had told her what his father said about coming over on Sunday, he went to find Bella so he could let her know Pluto would be staying with Haze and Dancie for a little while. He told her the whole story while she rolled out biscuit dough.

"I swear! Seem like that boy need a guardian angel perched on his shoulder to keep him out of trouble. Why, he was doing fine at the livery and now he have to go and aggravate 'em down there. Taking it upon himself to groom up that mule. Not bothering to ask could he borrow it." She dipped a jelly glass in flour and cut out little rounds of dough.

"He didn't mean any harm, Bella."

"Meaning harm and doing harm is two different things. On the other hand, I thank the Lord he got the news to yo' papa. Miss Eva was in a bad way. She perk up considerably when he come."

Bella gave a big sigh and shook her head as she

placed the biscuits in the pan one by one. "I don't rightly know if Pluto ought to come back here to Riley. What's gonna become of that boy? I swear, he don't seem able to take the easy way in things."

"He's a whole lot of fun to be with."

"Ain't it the truth?" Bella smiled, remembering. "He sho has pleasured his ole granny. It's gonna be a sorrow to me if he don't come back. I love that child and that's the gospel truth."

"But you've got so many grandchildren, Bella."

"You think that make some kind of difference?"

"I guess not," he answered, but he wasn't sure about that. If his mama had a whole lot of children, the loving and the worrying would get spread out. It wouldn't be the same. Anyway, Bella's grandchildren didn't have to be her salvation the way he did for his mother.

He went out on the back porch and sat down to think about it. Bella loved Pluto, and if he didn't come back, she'd be all by herself. She'd miss him a lot, it would be a sorrow, but it wouldn't kill her like it probably would his mother if he went off and didn't come back. He tried to imagine what his mother would be like without him. How it would be if he himself just never had been born? Suppose she never had married his daddy at all and hadn't the faintest idea about such a person as John Beaumont Greer. He tried to picture her selling piece goods in a store, not having any children to look after — to look after or to grieve over. Would she have needed somebody to be her salvation then? Who would it have been?

A horse came clattering across the side yard. Suddenly he was looking into the red face of a big man with an angry voice.

"You, boy! Is Miz Beaumont home?"

"Yes, sir," he said. "I'll go call her."

"Wait a minute. Maybe you're the one who can tell me the whereabouts of that crazy young nigger who ruined my mule and then ran off with him."

John's heart thumped against his ribs. Somehow he hadn't thought of this happening.

"No, sir. I can't." He crossed his fingers. He told himself that it wasn't a lie. He really couldn't tell, because Pluto was his friend.

"Can't or won't?" Mr. Garfield boomed. "I understand he's been working around here. You wouldn't be covering up for that black rascal, now would you?"

John had a feeling the man knew all the time, had maybe even seen him on Henry, and wanted to trap him in a lie. He blurted out, "I don't know what you're talking about. I'm just visiting here with my mama. She's real sick."

"You don't say. Well, let Miz Beaumont go about her nursing duties then. I wouldn't want to disturb the sick. Just tell her for me that I'm aiming to skin that boy alive if I catch him." He leaned down closer to John. "What's he doing around here anyhow? Comes from down near Treeola, I hear. I'd lay money he's running from trouble down there."

"I don't know, sir," he said, almost swallowing the

107

words, wishing he had it in him to say some sass like, "None of your blasted beeswax."

"Well, he better be long gone. She can tell him I said so." He wheeled the horse around and galloped out of the yard, leaving John relieved and mad and ashamed of himself all at the same time. He kept thinking of things he wished he had said. Then, after there wasn't any chance of being heard, he yelled, "You old stinkpot! I'll skin you alive yourself!" He started feeling shaky and sick at his stomach.

Bella came out and put her hand on his shoulder. "I thank you, child, for not telling where he's at. You better go let Miss Sally know what done happen." When he told Gran about Mr. Garfield and what Pluto had done to Henry, she didn't seem to think it was so awful. "What's he all fumed up for, I'd like to know. He got his mule back. Goodness knows it'll grow back all that hair and be just about as pretty a thing as it ever was."

But she explained that Mr. Garfield had it in for the Beaumonts ever since Grandpapa wrote pieces in his paper years ago about how it wasn't right for the commissaries to charge close to double the cash price for stuff poor tenant farmers had to buy on credit. People had to wait until they sold their cotton to get a little money so they could pay up. By then they'd run up such a bill they never could come out with anything left over to start in on the next year. Mr. Garfield owned a couple of commissaries, and folks claim that's how he got well-to-do, charging outlandish prices.

"Your grandfather had a fine way with words, but he was no great shakes as a businessman. He never was able to make the paper pay off the way it might have. A few years back Rip Garfield refused to make him a loan from the bank when he needed to fix up the printing press. His health had already begun to fail. He never was able to get out another issue. It grieved him. He'd wanted to keep it going so you and Bentley could take it over one day. Yes, Rip knows how to hold a grudge, all right."

"You think he might keep after Pluto for a good long while, Gran? Daddy said he'd probably cool off in a few days."

"Rip's not the cooling-off type, to my way of thinking. And of course he's got influence in town. I doubt he's going to let Shumway take Pluto back to work at the stable anytime soon."

He wanted to ask whether there was a chance Mr. Garfield might find out about the smashed windows down in Treeola, but it seemed like Gran didn't know anything about it, so he didn't bring it up.

That evening when he had supper with his mama on a makeshift table by her bed, he tried to think of something to say to cheer her up. He wished Pluto could have been there. He'd know how to make her feel better. He sure knew how to get along with people. It seemed like he knew everything — except book learning. Then a thought came into his head that was so unexpected he wanted to laugh. Mama was a real good teacher. Pluto was a real good learner. Maybe they could fit together. He started trying to tell her about Pluto in a way that would make her understand how special he was and how they were friends.

"And it looks like maybe he'll be staying out there for a while, so you can get to know him when we go back." Then, because he was afraid she was getting ready to say they might not be going, he added, "He sure needs somebody to teach him. Gran likes him a whole lot. She says he's smart as a whip."

"Sweetheart," she said, "I know you feel like it's home out there. But the fact is, we may have to stay here in town where I can earn some kind of money now that, well, you know, now that we don't have anything coming in."

He felt like she had punched him in the stomach, but he tried to sound calm and grown-up as he explained to her Papa's chances for the new church job, talking up the good points. "And cotton'll be ready for picking before long. Plutie and I can hire out."

She made a little disgusted sound. "We've not come to that, I hope. Sending my little boy into the fields like a . . ." She didn't finish, but he knew what she meant. It didn't make sense that it was all right for Pluto, but not for him. She went on. "When I'm stronger, I'll find work. I can help out in the dry goods store maybe. You can go to a good school finally.
110

You're certainly ready for that. Miss Polk tries her best, but Black Creek's not the place for an intelligent boy like you. We'll see your daddy on Sundays. It'll work fine. You'll see."

His supper was sitting in his middle like a brick.

"Daddy's going to be working awful long hours, Mama. He needs for you to be there to keep him from getting lonesome and down in the dumps. If he gets too terribly lonesome — gets to feeling real bad — he wouldn't eat right or anything. He might get sick. And you know what else he might do. Drink whiskey."

He hadn't meant to say all that just yet. He'd meant to wait until she was stronger. But there it was. She started to cry. She put down her fork and covered her face with her hands so that it was hard to make out what she was saying between sobs, but it was something like, "Don't you start at me, too. I just cannot take any more." He had to make it up to her. He didn't know how he could.

The room was hot and he thought with so much crying she must be about to burn up, so he took the palmetto fan lying on the bed and swooshed it back and forth. She held her face to get the breeze but the tears kept on coming. He had heard about people bleeding to death. He wondered if they could cry to death. He wished he knew how to say something about God. When Spud had died the preacher had said to lay all your cares on Jesus and let Him do the caring for you. But when John tried it out in his head,

111

it didn't feel right. It was like he was aiming to get out of doing whatever it was he ought to be doing himself. He had to say something.

"Please don't cry, Mama. We'll do whatever you want. I just made that up about Daddy drinking whiskey. He's not going to do that anymore. Ever. He said so. It's going to be all right. We'll stay here if you want. I won't make any fuss about it. We'll do whatever you say. Cross my heart."

Finally she quieted down and blotted her face with the napkin. "I'm sorry, son. Sit down and eat your supper. I'm doing my best to make some kind of sense out of things, but I guess I'm not up to it just yet."

She was acting like herself again, and she even ate a little more. John was relieved, of course, but it came to him that he'd paid a mighty high price. He couldn't let himself think about exactly what it was he had got himself into by swearing that. What he was giving up. He couldn't think about it. He just had to remember he was saving her life. Being her salvation.

"Want me to read to you out of the Bible?" he asked. That would take his mind up.

"Maybe later. Right now I just want to rest a little."

As he took the dishes back to the kitchen, Mr. Duff was sitting in the parlor. "Elgin?" he called. "Is that you?" Gran had told him that Elgin was the old man's brother who'd been dead nearly sixty years, but that once in a while the old man got mixed up and thought that's who he was waiting for. "Come in, come on in, for goodness sake. I have the dominoes all ready for a game."

Somebody had given Mr. Duff a special set with the dots poking out so he could feel them. It was his favorite thing in the whole world, now that he couldn't see to read. John had heard his grandmother complain about having to humor the old man by always letting him win. When Miss Rennie played she would beat him, and he would either get to feeling sorry for himself or accuse her of cheating.

"No, sir, this is me, John Beaumont," he answered, using the name Gran usually called him. He hoped the old man wouldn't ask him to play, but of course he did. John turned the lamp up, since his fingers couldn't figure out the dots by feel, and settled himself to do a kind deed. The old man smelled of sickness and it felt peculiar to be trying hard not to win. In spite of himself, the thought of home and Pluto slipped into his mind. He wondered what his friend was doing right that minute. Joking, laughing, having fun. He hoped his daddy was in on it. Tears stung his eyes but he blinked them back.

When the game was finally over and he was helping to put the pieces away, Mr. Duff said, "You're a bright young fellow. How would you like it if I let you play me another game tomorrow? Wouldn't that be dandy?"

John would just about as soon take a whipping as play again, but he knew he'd end up doing it, every time he was asked. And he knew the old man would probably ask him every night from now to kingdom come. Why couldn't he just say, "No, sir. I don't believe I'd care for another game"? And that would be the end of it. But it was awful to be old and nearly blind and muddled in the head.

"Yes, sir. That'd be nice," he said. He turned the lamp down low and walked the old man back to his room. He'd sworn he'd stay here and not make a fuss about it. But he hadn't sworn not to hate it.

11

 The next day Gran brought out a stack of old newspapers for John to look at. After a while he asked her, "You reckon it made much of a difference — all this stuff Grandpapa wrote? A difference in how poor folks got along, I mean?" He was thinking about Haze and Dancie, and especially Pluto.

"Oh, probably not a whole lot. Things are mighty slow to change, I'm afraid. Takes a lot of doing. Takes a long time. In his younger days he put a good deal of stock in that old saying, 'The pen is mightier than the sword.' But the way the sword swept across this land — the wretched violence — he almost gave up believing in that." She showed him the piece that had made Mr. Garfield so mad. It talked about "unbridled greed" and "ruthless ill-gotten gains."

"He used to write more in that vein, but then his language started to soften up. I'm partly responsible. I begged him to tone down. Things were in a tumult in the eighties, feelings running high. It wasn't out of the ordinary for newspaper people to get roughed

115

up, even shot, if their opinions weren't in line with everybody else's. Over in Freemont County in less than ten years' time they had three editors done in by violence."

A shiver went through John. Maybe that was what he ought to be, a brave newspaper editor who would stand up for the right and make things better. And it seemed like a sign that he and Pluto had already been talking about it.

"I been thinking, Gran. I might want to try running a paper. But maybe I'm not smart enough. I'm not anywhere near as smart as Bentley was." He thought she ought to know that.

"Oh, come now. Bentley was a bright child, but you have to remember he was getting better schooling than you've had. You'll be right as rain soon as you start to going here in town."

That was coming up again. What was the word Mrs. Plummer used about the school? Rigorous. The very sound of it gave him an all-gone feeling.

"You know Daisy Plummer, Gran?" He needed to know if she expected him to be like that.

"Well, yes!" Her voice made a pleased little up-and-down sound. "Emmaline's little girl. Of course. Would you like me to invite her to come over and play with you? Be friends? Wouldn't that be nice?"

"No'm!" he fairly shouted. He couldn't think of anything much worse. "I just mean she sounds awful smart. I'm pretty sure I wouldn't be able to keep up in that school."

"The very idea! You'll be the head of your class in no time."

He knew that was what she'd expect. It wasn't possible. He wasn't up to it. They'd find out how much there was he didn't know. They'd poke fun at him. Anyway he'd just made a friend and he wanted to be where Pluto was.

"And when you get your diploma from school here, I have it in my prayers for you to go on to college. Medicine or the law wouldn't be out of the question. It's heartbreaking what your father let happen to the money, but we'll find a way to manage. Your mama and I'll be so proud of you."

Why wouldn't she say his daddy would be proud, too? Why did she keep on acting like he didn't count?

"No'm. I don't think I'd take to it after all. I'll likely just stay out yonder at home. I druther raise mules." He didn't know if he meant it or not. He just wanted her not to treat his daddy like he didn't matter.

"What a way to talk. Well, it's been a trying time. Let's not discuss it anymore right now."

He went on looking through the newspapers, seeing if there was anything in them about colored people, wondering if his grandfather had ever written any pieces trying to make things better especially for them. He couldn't find much of anything. He read an article about what a fine place Riley was to live in, but that mostly had to do with white people — how the town was growing now to beat the band with a hotel, a bank, two cotton gins, and a school that any town in

117

the country could be proud of. He found a piece saying how fortunate folks were to live in such a healthful place, since the yellow fever that killed thousands of people up in Memphis never got there. They had to put guards up on all the roads and nobody could get into town or out without a permit. They couldn't bring in anything to sell from the places where the fever was bad.

The only time he found any mention of colored people was in an advertisement that bragged about a shop in town. "It has for many years supplied the tonsorial wants of Riley with promptness and efficiency." In his grandpapa's dictionary he found out that *tonsorial* meant 'connected with being a barber.' "The shop is supplied with all the conveniences such as a room for taking baths, a shoe-polishing department, and an up-to-date laundry. It is under the reliable management of Herbert Chambers, col." *Col.* meant 'colored,' of course. Like you couldn't let a colored person get his name in the paper without making it clear it wasn't a white person who was latched on to that name. It came to him that Pluto might come back to town and get a job there. He might like cutting hair and shaving whiskers better than roaching mules. Maybe the two of them could have a barbershop together some day. Then he wouldn't have to worry about getting all that rigorous education. He copied down the whole advertisement. When he saw Pluto he'd ask him if he wanted to be a tonsorial artist. If only old Mr. Garfield would cool off.

The next day was Sunday, when his daddy was coming. Church would have been too much of a strain for his mama, but Gran insisted on taking John. Maybe it was a good idea. He had a lot to ask for. For Mama to be so glad to see Daddy that she'd agree to go on back home. For Daddy to get the bricklaying job so there'd be enough money and some left over to buy mules. For Pluto to stay around and be his friend so they could grow up and have a barbershop together. For Mr. Garfield to go to a big revival service and get religion the way some people did so he'd quit his meanness and be kind to everybody, especially Pluto.

John thought they'd be going in the buggy, but Gran said it wasn't too far to walk. She slicked down his hair with water and checked to see if his ears were clean. She made him put on a tie and wear his long pants that were too short and his good shoes that squeaked. On the way they started to pinch, too, and they squeaked so loud when he and Gran went in that a little girl sitting on the aisle turned around to look at his feet, rolled her eyes, and shrugged. Gran guided him into the same pew and seated herself between him and the girl. John had an awful notion that this was going to turn out to be Daisy, because there behind the preacher, swaying from side to side as she played the pipe organ, sat Mrs. Plummer. Gran gave him a pleased look and a little wink and then reached over to pat the girl's hand before she bowed her head.

John had been in this church lots of times before, mostly for funerals. But the thing he always remembered about it, aside from the quivery deep sound of the organ, was the way the sunshine through the stained glass windows made little blobs of color everywhere. Once when the prayer was very long, he had watched an orange blob move slowly across his knees and onto the polished oak pew before the preacher got to the Amen.

It wasn't the rector doing the preaching today but a somebody visiting, an older man who had lots of gray hair sprouting out behind a very high forehead. Now and then he would close his eyes, lift his head, and touch the tips of his fingers to his forehead as if he had to ease out some of the thoughts crammed in there. John had a hard time keeping track of all he was saying until the word "salvation" jumped out at him, like somebody had called him by name.

"Salvation. That is what our weary souls cry out for. Yes, salvation in the midst of life's tribulations." His voice would be low and rumbly one minute, and the next it would reach up high and come sliding down, separating the words into little pieces, then turning loud and sharp. "We seek it. Oh, how we seek it, everywhere, everywhere, except in the one place where it can surely be found, brothers and sisters. *He* is our rock and our only salvation, and oh, how bitterly we go astray when we think we can find it an-y oth-er place!"

John wondered if his mama had ever heard about this. He wondered how he could tell her. He couldn't just go in and say, "Mama, maybe you don't know it, but God is your salvation, not me." It needed all of the preacher's fine and powerful way of putting it, or it sounded flat, like he was just trying to get out of the responsibility. Maybe he could learn to talk like that with lots of ups and downs, louds and softs.

They stood up to sing a hymn. He didn't know it, but it was all about being saved, so he tried to follow along with Gran. Once when the tune was going up, he kept right on up when everybody who knew it dropped back down. His wrong note hung there in the air, and the girl leaned forward again to roll her eyes some more. He couldn't stand her.

He had looked up *hippopotamus* in the dictionary and thought if he did have to talk with her he'd start right off asking her if she still didn't know how to spell that word that stumped her in the spelling bee. But he had a feeling she'd come back at him with something that was worse.

Sure enough, when it was over, Gran introduced him to Daisy, leaving out his last name the way she so often did. "John Beaumont's my one and only grandson, Daisy, and I'm hoping it won't be too long before he's a member of your class at school."

"Oh, really?" she answered, with a sappy sweet expression as long as Gran was looking at her. "How nice."

All he could think of to say was, "Have y'all had fractions yet?"

"Fractions? Oh, my, yes! We started ages ago. I think they're the greatest fun, don't you?"

121

He wondered if she was making it up. Arithmetic was his best subject, but Miss Polk had said fractions were something he wasn't quite ready to undertake.

"Are you and your mother walking home, Daisy?" Gran asked. "We'll just wait for Emmaline to put her music away if you are." Daisy smirked a little "Yessum," and John knew why they hadn't come in the buggy. Gran had this in mind all along. His feet hurt and Daisy was every bit as awful as he had expected. When Gran moved away to say hello to somebody, Daisy giggled and said, "I declare, your singing voice squeaks worse than your shoes do."

For a moment he was the little frazzle of nothing he turned into when anybody made fun of him like that, but suddenly it came to him to play like he was really Pluto. He knew right off the sort of thing Pluto would come up with at a time like that, so he put his fists on his hip bones and cocked his head and said, "Ain't it the truth! I plum forgot to oil up my singing apparatus before I left home."

It made all the difference. He felt full of himself again instead of a poor pitiful blob anybody could squash. When Daisy made a little disgusted sound he even had the nerve to say, "I sure would like to get shed of these here shoes."

"What a boor! My mother told me. You live way out in the country." She made it sound like something to be ashamed of. "You aren't really civilized. You probably haven't had shoes on all summer until today. You play with nigras, too." That did it.

122

"But I can spell *hippopotamus*," he said. "That's more than some people can." He hobbled outside and sat down on the grass to take off his shoes. She followed him.

"Oh-h, you think you're so smart, don't you! Just wait. You just wait. You'll find out what an enormous number of things you don't know. Why, I'll bet you haven't the faintest idea what . . . what" — her eyes blinked as she was trying to pick which of the enormous number of things she was going to hit him with — "what a . . . what a *conundrum* is. Or how long your intestines would be if they were stretched out. Do you?" He didn't. He wasn't a bit sure he wanted to know. "Ha! They'll put you back in the primer when you try going to a real school. You'll see!"

He couldn't think of any kind of comeback. That was too close to what he was most scared of.

When the two ladies came, Gran acted shocked that he'd taken off the pinching shoes, but Mrs. Plummer let out her little tinkly laugh and said, "John's simply a lad with his feet on the ground, Miss Sally." And she looked around for everybody to appreciate what she'd said.

Daisy put on her adorable manners and said, "Oh, Mrs. Beaumont, you know boys will be boys, alas!"

Then they all walked part of the way home together, but it was the ladies who did all the talking. He wished he'd made it clearer in his prayers that he never wanted to go to school in Riley.

123

*   *   *

As they walked on home, Gran left him alone about
Daisy and forgave him for taking off his shoes at
church when she saw the blister on one of his toes.
"My lands, will you look at that. We'll have to wash
it good and put a dab of salve on it when we get
home. I was planning to send you on down to the
livery to fetch Maud so your father could take you
and Mama out for a buggy ride and maybe a picnic
this afternoon. The change might do her good. You
reckon if we tied your toe up in a clean rag there'd
be any more walking left in those poor feet?"

The very idea of a picnic made his feet feel better
right away. When they got to the house one of his
father's mules was tied up at the hitching post. He
would have rushed on in, but Gran said to let the two
of them have a little talking time first. He didn't know
whether that meant that Gran was starting to be nicer
to his daddy or whether she knew Mama would be
explaining that she never was going back with him.
He got his toe tended to and took off.

He was nervous for a couple of reasons. One was
that Mr. Shumway would ask him questions about
Pluto. The other was that even though he was only
going to walk Maud down the street, there was always
a chance she might rear up or run off or snap at him.
He wished he wasn't such a baby about horses and
mules. He knew very well that Maud was old and
gentle and wouldn't do any of those things, but his
mind was so far into the worrying habit that it didn't

124

seem able to stop. He'd just have to put up with it and go along about his business.

As it turned out, Mr. Shumway wasn't even there, it being Sunday, and Jesse insisted on coming along himself, saying, "Miss Sally got nobody to do for her now since that no-count Pluto done run off. I better go see does she want me to split a little kindling wood."

"You just want to get yourself a plate of Sunday dinner, I bet," John said to himself, wishing he had the nerve to say it out loud to Jesse for saying Pluto was no-account. Wishing he could say, "Henry wouldn't have that chopped-off mane if you hadn't been so skunk drunk on whiskey."

As Jesse was leading Maud down the road he noticed John's tied-up toe and offered to help him up on the horse. "Don't be scared of ridin' bareback. This here ole mare be too lazy to buck anybody off."

Rather than come right out and say he never had been on a horse, bareback or not, John made up a story about a boil on his bottom so big he couldn't sit right. Then he felt terrible that he'd gone and told a lie right after he'd been to church. Maybe it ruined all the good he'd done. As he trailed along behind Jesse and Maud, he whispered, "Please keep Mama and Daddy together," walking in time with the words, saying it over and over, until he felt in a daze.

When they got back his mama had her regular clothes on, and she and his daddy were sitting on the front porch holding one another's hand. That was a

125

good sign. Gran had fixed a fried chicken picnic for them to take and after Jesse hitched up the buggy she brought out pillows to make Mama comfortable, along with an old bedspread for the ground. Papa lifted Mama into the seat and off the three of them went, heading for a grove of pecan trees at the edge of town where it was shady and there was a spring nearby for getting water. On the way his father told him that he was starting the bricklaying job the next morning. And Haze and Dancie wanted Pluto to stay on and hire out to one of the planters when cotton was ready to pick. That meant months of work.

John tried not to let the grin he was feeling spread over his whole face. For starters, God was doing just fine in answering his prayers.

"Now all we've got to do, son, is to convince the old sweet mama here that we can make ends meet without her going to work in town."

"That's a six-month job at most, Joe. We have to think ahead. Be sensible, now. I know I can get something to do. John and I should stay put right here, at least until you see what comes up next for you after the church is finished."

God was not doing so well after all. It was like somebody had set down a big strawberry shortcake in front of him just long enough to get his mouth to watering and then snatched it away. Pluto would be living right in his back yard, and he'd be going to school with the likes of Daisy Plummer, having to put up with Miss Rennie and old Mr. Duff day in and day out. There had to be another way.

"Hey, I got an idea, Mama," he said. "I betcha there's some stores you could work at in Crawford. Then you could ride in along with Daddy every morning."

His father shook his head. "That wouldn't do, son. I told you what long hours they're making the builders put in. Twelve hours every day, plus a long ride in and out. Your mama's a strong woman, but that's beyond reason."

They rode past the two-story brick building. It looked huge and hungry to John, like the enormous red bull he had bad dreams about sometimes. There was a different room for every grade, and out front was a concrete walk through the playground and a long railing for tethering the animals country children rode in on.

"Just look there, son. See what a fine school you'll be going to?" his mama said. "This wasn't here when I was growing up. You're very lucky to have such an opportunity."

What he wanted to say was, "I can get every bit of the learning I want at Black Creek, Mama. I'll read lots and learn everything I need to know. Please let's go back home." But since he'd sworn not to make a fuss, he didn't say anything.

"Son," said his daddy, "your mama's exactly right. Why, if I'd had a chance to go to a school like this when I came along, I might be making a better living for all of us today." He turned to his wife. "But in another year or so, Eva, John can saddle up and ride in, the way Bentley used to. And we can all keep on being a family together."

She shook her head. "You get started on your new job. We can put off deciding until next Sunday. Please, Joe, let's not talk about it for now, just for now. Let's us enjoy this outing. I'm so relieved to see blue sky over me instead of that sad old water stain on Mama's wall." So they rode on and had a picnic in the shade of the pecan trees. John's daddy told how on Friday he and Pluto had mixed up a whole batch of mortar and practiced with the bricks they found lying around under the house. They'd make a little wall out of them and then tear it down while the mortar was still wet so he could practice again, getting used to the feel of the trowel.

"Pluto rode over to Crawford with me on Saturday, and I tell you that boy sure has a knack for keeping a person's spirits up. 'Mister Joe,' he'd say, 'they bound and obliged to snatch you up and give you that job. They be lucky to get somebody can lay so straight and smooth. They gonna say, "Hire on that Mr. Joe Greer right quick before he get a better offer!" ' I'm no hot shot bricklayer, but I walked in there pretty sure of myself."

"He's real good with mules, too, Daddy."

"I'll say. Takes to 'em about as much as I do. Kept me talking mules most of the way home."

John could imagine it. Somehow it made him feel funny. He was glad Pluto and his daddy got along so well, but if they took to liking each other all that much, they might not have enough liking left over for him. He supposed what he felt was jealous. One day he heard Amelia Thompson at school tell Hosie Reed he was acting jealous because she'd been nice to somebody else. Well, it said in the Bible that God was a jealous God. He'd heard that lots of times. Maybe God felt that uneasy, heavy way when he saw people getting too friendly with the devil. But it sure didn't feel good. What John needed was for them all to get back home and be in their rightful place, with him his daddy's only boy and Pluto's best friend. Mama would be there looking after everything.

When they had finished eating the fried chicken and pie and drinking the lemonade, Mama told John where to find the spring she remembered from coming here when she was a girl. He was supposed to go wet a napkin so they could wipe their sticky fingers. He found it right where she said it would be, bubbling up and trickling over the side of the rock. It had been running out like that since before he was born, probably before his mama and daddy were born, without anybody doing the pumping.

He stood watching it for a long time, listening to the small gurgling sound, out of sight of his mama and daddy. Maybe they were kissing. A dragonfly hummed over his head and he looked up to see it

129

hanging there against the hot blue sky, its wings a blur. Maybe it was an angel. Maybe it was a messenger of God.

"We got to go back home. All three of us. We just got to. Tell Him."

He took the soaked napkin and headed back. A blue jay swooped down over his path, cawing at him as if he didn't have any right to be there, and a feather fluttered to the ground in front of him. As he picked it up he knew it was important, but it took him a moment to think why. Then he remembered.

One day when he and Mama had been sitting out in front on the grass, waiting for Bentley to get home from school, a lady had driven up in a buggy and asked if she could come show them something. They didn't get much in the way of company, so Mama said to get out and come right on over. The lady had a book in one hand and in the other she had a blue jay feather. She'd handed it to John and asked him what color he saw. Then she made him look again, holding it up against the sky. There wasn't a scrap of blue in it any longer. He and Mama both were surprised.

It turned out the lady was down from Memphis selling encyclopedias and she showed them where in her book they could have found out about color in blue jay feathers and why it was like that. The book was chock full of interesting things. She said it was one of a set they could buy and keep so they could look up anything a person would ever need to know, or just *want* to know because it was a part of God's wondrous world.

Mama had fixed the lady a cup of coffee and kept her talking until Bentley got home so he could see the beautiful book. She wanted Daddy to see it, too, so they could talk about buying a set, but the lady couldn't wait that long. She was going around that week to stir up interest, she said, and would be back in a week or so to take orders. She gave them some papers telling the particulars.

That night Mama and Daddy decided there was no way they could pay for the encyclopedias right then, but the lady never came back, anyway. Later somebody said she might have got the yellow fever when it hit Memphis so bad.

He just handed the feather to his mama after she'd wiped her sticky fingers. He didn't say anything, waiting to see if she got the connection. He had never forgotten, but maybe she had. She sat stroking the feather for a while, and then she grinned and said, "Joe! Tell me what color you see."

"Well, I'd say what we've got here is a gray jay feather," he said, holding it to the light. "See how smart I am?" And they all laughed.

"You could sell books, Mama, like that lady! You could live back at home and go out selling to folks all over the county. I could go along with you in the wagon to help, or maybe Pluto if I'm in school!" The words tumbled over each other. "Remember how everybody liked those books? You could make a lot of money. Wouldn't that be fine?"

"Take it easy, son. We agreed with your mama we weren't going to talk about the future while we're on our picnic."

But it didn't matter. He could tell she was thinking about what he'd said even though they were talking about other things. She seemed lighthearted and started teasing Daddy about a picnic they'd been on long ago.

"Your daddy had taken a shine to me, or so he says, but he was too shy to ask if he could walk me home. He just kept doing tricks to see if I'd notice him. Walking on his hands, if you please, with his feet waving in the air like cornstalks."

"Your mama was the prettiest girl there. All the fellows were after her. I had to do something. I wasn't much of a talker, but I was young and limber. She walked home with somebody else anyhow."

"Show me, Daddy! Show how you walked on your hands."

"I'm not so young and limber anymore, sad to say."

But he held John's feet straight up and let him have a try. When he turned loose John flopped to the ground and hit so that the blister on his toe popped. The rag had long since come off and the stinging of it made him yell and then moan a little. Then a curious thing happened. Or didn't happen, actually. Mama didn't jump up and come running to see if he was all right.

132

Part of him felt sorry for himself. She didn't care if he was hurting. Another part of him knew it was a good sign.

Later he and Daddy picked her an armful of black-eyed Susans, and they went back home. Gran took Mama in to lie down and take a rest, while John and his daddy unhitched Maud and gave her a drink. When they got inside Mama was already talking to Gran about how she might sell books. "It would be a lot better than spending the rest of my days here in town cutting off piece goods for folks. I could sell all kinds of books, not just encyclopedias. Books with stories and poems."

He wished Mama had talked to Daddy about it first. It looked like she was going to let Gran make up her mind for her. And Gran was looking pinch-mouthed. His mother reached over and took his hand. "John here found a feather like the lady used that time to get our curiosity up. Remember, son? She had a nice dignified appearance, but lively, too. You'd have liked her, Mama."

Since they wouldn't bring his father into the discussion, he did it himself. "What do you think, Daddy?"

"Selling's not easy work, son. And I sure wouldn't want your mama traipsing around the countryside by herself."

"I should think not!" said Gran.

"No! Pluto and me could go with her."

"Pluto and *I*," his mother said. "But you'll be in school, learning to talk good English."

"I guess a lot of folks were taken with those books that time. You came close to talking me into buying some, didn't you, hon? I'd give you credit for knowing how to sell all right," said his father.

"If this *should* turn out to be a possibility — and I'm not a bit convinced that it is — right here in Riley would be the appropriate place to try to sell. No sense in traveling all around," said Gran.

"Aw, no!" John cried out, almost before he realized he was going to say anything. "Oh, I wouldn't think so. In town folks can just go down to the schoolhouse or somewhere and look things up. It's out in the country where it's hard to find what you need to know. It's out there where selling would be a heap easier."

"You could find out who's interested in town, Mama, and I could drive in and try to sell to them, too. I'd have both places for my territory." Mama was getting shiny-eyed and rosy-cheeked. But then she caught her breath. "How on earth would I ever find the name of that book company? Joe, you reckon we might still have the papers the lady gave us that time?"

"I doubt it, hon, but we could see."

"What's the matter with me!" Mama cried, sitting up and swinging her legs over the side of the bed. "Why in the world didn't I think about the good old *Laurel Library*? It's a big book your grandpapa used, John, down at the newspaper office, whenever he needed to look up anything. Mama, do you know where it is?"

"Just hold your horses for about two shakes of a lamb's tail," said Gran, and she went and got an enormous raggedy book that she dusted off and put down on the bed beside Mama.

"See, son. This is the book I used many a time when I was in school. It has everything under the sun a person could want to know." Excited, every bit of the sadness gone, she turned through the pages, and some of them came loose. "I guess somehow I always connected it with the printing press and didn't think of it as something people should have in their homes. I do believe I might make a go of selling such as this. Oh, here it tells about John Greenleaf Whittier. Isn't that a lovely name? The Quaker poet. He wrote that beautiful poem I've read to you many a time, son. The one about snow. Remember?" She flipped more pages. "Oh, and here's something I wrote a report on one time — redwood trees. It tells about these enormous trees they have in California, big enough to cut a tunnel and drive a wagon through with the tree still standing. Trees right there today that were full grown when Jesus was a little boy. Think about that!"

John thought about it, but it didn't seem as wonderful as the new way his mother was being today. She kept on. "Somewhere in here it tells all about dinosaurs that used to live on the earth, before there were people . . . and about the planets up in the sky. Your grandpapa loved to think about the planets. Oh, everybody will want to have a book like this. This one's falling apart, but I'll bet you they've printed up

135

something new and even better. It tells here in the front where it came from. Chicago, Illinois. I'm going to write them a letter. Except there's no street address. Oh, dear."

"Never mind," Gran said. "We'll find it. We can go through all your father's papers. Time and again I've thought to throw out and burn all that stuff. He kept everything. There'll be some kind of receipt for that book."

So Gran was won over. She even offered the buggy for the undertaking, saying that she didn't use it enough to make keeping it worth while. Just so they'd come take her out to the country now and then. It was all happening so fast and fine that John felt dizzy. Maybe sometime he and Pluto both could go out selling with Mama. Maybe she could get Pluto to reading out of those encyclopedias, and he'd have all the book learning a person could ever need.

In the late afternoon Mama kissed his daddy goodbye and said they'd come to a decision the next weekend, but John felt like it was as good as settled. They'd go home and she'd make money selling books. He picked up the feather and went to the front yard to wave his daddy off. The Lord sure did move in mysterious ways, all right. He felt on top of the world.

12

He was still in good spirits after his daddy had ridden off, until what happened later that evening. He was in the kitchen with Bella, telling her all about the big plans for Mama to start selling books when she was stronger. Of course, they talked about Pluto, too.

"Mr. Joe had mighty nice things to say about that boy. Lord knows I miss him, but it's gonna work fine for him to stay out yonder a while with Haze and Dancie. Good for him, good for them. Dancie had a hard time in her growing up. She never wanted no child of her own. But I bet Plutie done got on her good side right quick."

"They sure took to one another. He could even make her laugh and that ain't easy to do."

Right then they heard a noise on the back porch. It was Jesse and there was no way of telling how long he'd been there.

"Evenin', Miss Bella. Young man. How y'all feelin' this fine evenin'?"

"Tolerable, Jess. What you up to?" Bella didn't seem a bit glad to see him.

"Well," he said and stopped, slapping his hat at a spider high up on the wall, not letting Bella catch his eye. "I figured I ought to let you know 'bout somethin'. See, Mr. Rip Garfield come by the livery and he done offer me two bits if I was to find out where he could lay his hands on Pluto. Two bits sho would go a long ways towards easin' my thirst, but I ain't told him a blessed thing, Miss Bella. 'Ceptin' I did allow he probably just gone back home to his mama." He leaned down and scooped the dead spider, taking his time as he dropped it over the edge of the porch. "I figured you might want to give me a little somethin' for not making no trouble for y'all."

With that, he turned and looked Bella straight in the eye. Neither of them moved for a while. Then Bella said, "Uh-huh. That was mighty kind of you, Jesse, but a dime is all the money I got on me." While she was looking in her pocketbook for the handkerchief it was tied up in, John ran to get what was left of his candy. There were only four winding balls left, but Jesse acted pleased and even generous, offering a piece back to John and one to Bella, but they wouldn't touch it. As he stood there making sucking noises and clicking the hard candy against his teeth, Bella fixed him a sugar biscuit.

"You better get on home now, Jesse. Take this here along to keep you company. Much obliged for coming by. I know I can count on you to do the right thing."

After he'd left John asked, "You think Jesse might get so thirsty he'd take the two bits?"

"Ain't no need to worry, child," Bella said, sitting down to put on her going-home shoes. "If Mr. Garfield want to find Pluto so bad, he's gonna find him. He ain't fixin' to pay that worthless Jesse no two bits. That nigger stood out there and heard us in here talkin' 'bout Haze and Dancie, most likely. He made all that up. He plays folks off against one another. Been doin' it all his born days."

"Pluto's real good at watching out for himself, anyhow. And he's in a safe place. My daddy and Haze and Dancie won't let anything happen to him, will they?"

"Not if they can help it."

"They all like him a lot. Dancie's treating him like he was hers." Then, "What did you mean about she didn't ever want any children?"

"Well, she come from a family that never was able to lay low when they feelin's got riled. And a heap of things happened that be hard for anybody to take. Dancie lost a daddy and a brother to the Klan."

John knew a little bit about the Ku Klux Klan. Things were whispered at school and when he had asked at home, Mama had said it was born of sad necessity after the war when the carpetbaggers from up North were ruining the South, coming down to take advantage of the terrible confusion and destruction everywhere after the Confederacy lost the war. But now it was white trash carrying on and doing dreadful things, giving it a bad name.

"You mean the Klan killed them? What would they do a thing like that for?"

"Little boy, don't you know nothin'?" Bella looked at him, shaking her head. "White folks got awful mean when it looked like the colored was gettin' 'round to believin' they done quit bein' slaves. They start to act like they be free and here come nightriders commencin' to swarm all over, flappin' like spooks, burnin' crosses, burnin' up people's houses. If such as that don't do the job, they got worse ways."

She stood up and tied her head rag on. He didn't know what to say. He certainly couldn't just say he was sorry. He didn't say anything.

"Dancie told Haze way back before they married she ain't willin' to cause one more child to come into the world and have to put up with such." Bella was ready to go, already at the door.

"Plutie told me about his brother." He wanted her to know that the two of them were friends in spite of everything. "And all about the window, too."

She turned quickly and put her finger to her lips.

"I wouldn't tell," he whispered. "You know I'd never tell, no matter what. But he's going to be all right. You'll see." John felt like he had got God to pay attention today, since so many other things were coming out right. It was fine to know that he was maybe the cause of Pluto being looked after. He wanted her to know. "I prayed the Lord about him in church today."

Bella looked down at him, her lips tight in an up-side-down smile. She nodded slowly and took him by the hand to pull him closer to her. "And I was doin' the very same." He could smell the good mixture of sweat and dishwater and a smell like pine needles and fresh baked bread as she let in a deep breath and closed her eyes. "Sweet Jesus, you have told us where two are gathered in your blessed name you are gonna be right there amongst them. We ask you, Lord, to shine your light upon the path of Pluto Johnson and guard his ways and bring him to your Kingdom by and by. This boy and me, we ask you that. We trust him to your care and keepin', this day and all the days to come. Amen."

It was some of the best praying he'd ever heard, and he went to bed that night feeling sure it was all going to work out all right, even though something made him remember the dream Pluto had had about the bloodhounds and it kept him awake for a good long while.

John spent a lot of his time during the following week reading the *Laurel Library* in the parlor with the shades pulled down to keep out the sun. A scorching heat wave was smothering everything, and his blistered foot worried Mama just enough for her to tell him to stay inside and keep it out of the dirt. She was certainly changing her ways. She never mentioned getting blood poisoning although that was what she was usually afraid blisters were coming to. John supposed it was because she had something else to think about besides what bad things might happen to him.

Most things were slowing down from the heat, but not Mama and Gran. They fanned and unbuttoned the top buttons of their blouses as they sifted through old papers until they found the address they needed. Gran went to see the head schoolmaster to find out about some more books and companies, but she went early before the sun got too fierce. When she got back she unbuttoned again and put a handkerchief dampened with violet water around her neck as she and Mama wrote letters. Then they even started making up a list of people who might turn into customers.

Being a natural-born worrywart, John gave some thought to Jesse and Mr. Garfield, but not a lot. After Bella's prayer it was easier to turn Pluto over to the Lord, for care and keeping, like she said, especially since there didn't seem to be a blessed thing he could do anyhow.

One of the first subjects he looked up in the huge book was intestines. He found out that they came in two sizes, large and small, and that the length of the small ones curled around in the insides of the average grown person was twenty-three feet, which he never would have believed if somebody had told him. But there it was in a book. You had to believe it. Close by was a drawing of the human body, telling what all the different muscles were called. He spent a good while trying to learn to say the name of the longest one there, the sternocleidomastoideus. If he ended up having to go to church again next Sunday, he might just say to Daisy Plummer, "Good morning. How's your sternocleidomastoideus today?" But then it occurred to him that Daisy's family might own a *Laurel Library*, too. Maybe that was how come she knew so much about intestines, from reading right here in the same place. And it stood to reason, she'd look up the longest word there so she could show off.

He gave up and looked for something else. Pluto's name. Why hadn't he gone straight to that? Right after they met, Pluto had asked what John knew about the god he was named for. He found the place, and it told about how three brother gods drew straws to see who would be in charge of the universe. Neptune got the sea, Jupiter got the heavens, and Pluto got the dark underworld, where he ruled over the dead people and was very rich since he was also in charge of all the precious metals hidden deep in the earth. He owned a helmet that made whoever had it on invisible. John thought that was exactly what Pluto needed in case of a run-in with old Mr. Garfield.

He couldn't wait to see Pluto's face when he told him all this about himself. How his name stood for the god of the underworld, who ruled over dead folks and all kinds of treasure. Such an interesting piece of information! And here it had been in this musty old book for years and years just waiting for somebody to come along and open up to this page so it could get read about.

He wished he could find a piece telling the best way to pick cotton fast. Plenty of times, he had picked a few handfuls of the soft white puffs, pulling them loose from the dried pods and then picking out the hard little seeds that wanted to stay wrapped snug in the cotton. Of course the cotton gin did that but he'd been doing it just for fun. And picking for only as long as it was fun. But Pluto would be dragging a sack across his shoulders up and down the rows from daylight to dark, or as the colored people said, from can see to cain't. Before he went to bed he would have filled the bag more than once, emptying it on the scales each time and ending up picking almost as many pounds of cotton as he weighed himself, getting his pay by the pounds. Now that Mama had her mind taken up with other things, she might let him have a go at it. He wondered how long he would last.

The week dragged by as he waited for it to be Sunday, when he felt sure they'd be going home and he'd be in his rightful place finally, in his own room, with things the way they used to be, only better, with a friend living close by. So he read a lot and after supper, before dark, he'd go for a walk with Mama, who was getting stronger every day. He was careful not to say anything against being there at Gran's. He was going to abide by what he swore, but it was a world easier now that it looked like God was getting him out of Riley pretty soon.

One day the heat was even fiercer than usual. At sunup John was already damp with sweat and by noon his shirt was wringing wet. The porch steps burned his bare feet and Mama wouldn't let him crawl under the house to look for a cool spot in the dry powdery dust. But in the early afternoon it came to him to ask her to read the snow poem out loud, the way she sometimes read it at home for him and his daddy when it was blazing hot. It told about a big snowstorm up north somewhere and just listening to it you could think yourself into being cooler.

He'd seen snow twice. All he could remember from the first time was how he'd thought pieces of the sky were tearing loose, and he'd hidden under the covers and Bentley had teased him. Bentley wasn't around the second time, but it was close to Christmas and his little cousin Stella was visiting. His daddy had tied a piece of rope to an apple crate and pulled them skidding around the yard. Stella had been scared and so he'd been extra brave. Mama came out and threw snowballs at Daddy and they all ate snow ice cream. He could hardly sleep that night for wanting it to be morning, but it rained before dawn and when he woke up there wasn't a speck of white anywhere. It was like it never had happened. In the poem it was wonderful.

The snow kept on going for days, and there was so much of it the people couldn't get out of the house to go anywhere. He'd learned a little of it by heart and thought about standing up and saying it in school some day.

Mama said it was a fine idea, reading about snow, before they all got heat prostration, so she found the poem in one of Grandpapa's books, one called *Poetry Treasures for Young Folks*, which Mama and Gran had already decided might be a good seller. John carried straight chairs out to the shade of the cedar tree, and Gran called Mr. Duff to come listen, too, as Mama read all about the blizzard and icicles and shivering with cold.

Mr. Duff started to look perky, and when Mama finished he recited another poem he knew about snow. John could hardly believe the old man could remember so much, and his voice began to remind him of the preacher's. "Announced by all the trumpets of the sky arrives the snow, and driving o'er the fields . . ." The fine-sounding words poured out of his mouth, making sense all the way through without getting sidetracked and confused the way his talk sometimes did. When he had finished everybody felt as cool as if a breeze had sprung up, but there was no stopping Mr. Duff. He took off with "The Midnight Ride of Paul Revere" and remembered every word of it. John thought it must be grand to have so much stored up in your head. When the old man finally ran dry, John took the copy of *Poetry Treasures for Young*

Folks off to his favorite spot behind the chicken house and learned some more of "Snowbound" by heart.

Later that night, after the game of dominoes, which was a regular after-supper occurrence now, he was feeling sticky hot and itchy and out of sorts from the game. Nobody else seemed to be around at the moment, and he thought it might cool him down and ease him if he went out on the front porch and said some of the poem to himself. He was careful not to let the screen door bang so nobody would know he was out there. He went to the top of the porch steps and looked out into the darkness. He imagined that a lot of people had come to listen to him recite, everybody from Black Creek and maybe people from Riley school, even. He didn't let his voice get too loud, but he put lots of expression in it, trying for ups and downs like the preacher he'd heard Sunday, sweeping his arms up and out on the part about the sun and moon.

" 'The sun that brief December day, rose cheerless over hills of gray, And darkly circled, gave at noon, a sadder light than waning moon.' "

"My stars!" A voice came from out of the darkness. "What's all that about?" It was Miss Rennie, of course. As his eyes got used to the dim light, he could make out her shape sitting down at the far end of the porch. He could have kicked himself for not checking to see if anybody was there.

"I didn't know I was going to catch a show when

I came out here to catch the breeze." She laughed her hiccuppy laugh. "Here all this time you've been such a quiet little boy. I never knew you had it in you to be an actor feller. Do some more." He could just imagine her telling about it tomorrow down at the post office.

"It's for school," he said. "I have to practice."

"Aw, go on! I never heard tell of any kind of school in the middle of July. College maybe. You don't happen to go to college, now do you?"

Miss Rennie thought she was a great tease. She'd seem surprised that people got upset when she just wouldn't let them alone. "You know me, I'm such a tease," she'd say.

In bed that night he thought about what a miserable life it would be if he did end up having to live under the same roof with Miss Rennie. He tried to think of how Pluto would deal with somebody like her. Pluto would make you think he was having the time of his life if somebody snuck up on him and caught him reciting. John remembered how he'd suddenly pretended he was Pluto when he was with Daisy and how things changed for the better. He wondered if he could think himself into being Pluto whenever he needed to. It would be the next best thing to having a helmet that made him turn invisible.

At dinnertime, the following day, sure enough, Miss Rennie started in on him again. "Looka here, Miz Beaumont. You've been keeping secrets from us. It never dawned on me you and Miz Greer were raising this boy to go on the stage."

John felt like sliding under the table, but instead he caught himself in time and shifted right into playing like he was Pluto. "Aw, shucks, Miss Rennie. Here you go letting the cat out of the bag. Nobody was supposed to know about it yet." Then, before she could say anything, he turned to Gran and Mama. "She heard me out practicing some of my show last night."

"Is that so?" Gran said, not letting Miss Rennie see that all this surprised her as much as it probably did. "Last I heard, you were dickering between going to raise mules and going to write for a paper." Mama was watching him with a peculiar look but she wasn't saying a word.

"Oh, I expect I'll do both of those things, one time or another. But I've been giving some thought to going around reciting pieces, maybe doing musical numbers in between. Show folks a fine time."

"You plan on playing your grandpapa's violin?" Gran asked, looking like you might have knocked her over with a feather.

"No'm. I had it in mind I might take to studying on the harmonica. Daddy got me one in Memphis, Mama. I think I'd like that." It was as if he could hear Pluto saying the words right along with him. "I could travel all over the country in one of those tents that go around putting on shows, you know."

Mr. Duff piped up. "What's that? Chautauqua meeting come to town? I attended such an evening last week, in St. Louis, I believe it was. Very educational. I wouldn't want to miss it."

"No, there's not one coming, Mr. Duff," Gran said, helping him to another serving of mashed potatoes and gravy. "It was just the subject of general conversation."

"Well, now, I'll tell you what!" whooped Miss Rennie. "It just so happens some of the ladies in town are getting up a minstrel show down at the schoolhouse to raise money for one thing or another. Those shows are always a scream. They're calling this one 'Maids of Corkville,' from the cork they use to black up their faces, you see. I'll bet you a pretty they could use a talented actor like you, John. They might let you be a cute little nigger boy in the show. How does that strike you?"

He wanted to call her a stinkpot, the same as he'd called Mr. Garfield that time, except right to her face. He wanted to tell her she'd used a word he was nice enough never to say. But neither of those was Pluto's style. So what he said instead was, "Shoot! I got a better idea! I might could get you a real colored boy for the show, one that's plenty talented. Wouldn't need any face blacking from cork a-tall."

Miss Rennie laughed and threw up her hands. "Land sakes! This boy's been out there in the country way too long. I guess he never has seen a minstrel show in all his born days."

"You mean the whole thing is white people just making like they aren't white while they're up on the stage carrying on? I don't see why that's so funny. Sounds pretty dumb to me."

"Don't be rude, son," murmured his mother.

"Oh, you just don't know," Miss Rennie continued. "I like to have died laughing at the last one. Watching those fine cultured ladies sashaying around and singing like colored folks."

He was glad she didn't say "niggers" at least. "I sure wouldn't pay my good money to go see a thing like that. You reckon colored people ever put chalk on their faces and pretend they're white folks and all the colored people come and laugh at them? Maybe that's what I'll have as part of my show."

At that Gran hushed him up and declared she didn't know what had got into him. Mama reached out and felt his forehead and made him go lie down for a while. She said he certainly wasn't himself.

That was the gospel truth. As he lay on the cot beginning to feel more like himself he could hardly believe he had talked like that, cocky and full of devilment when he sort of melted into the picture of Pluto he had in his head. Once in a while his usual self felt that way, not scared of a living soul, but that was when he was off playing by himself, thinking his thoughts. When other people were around they were liable to make him feel squashed and mushy or else they would start expecting so much out of him that he was pure miserable from thinking how he was

151

obliged to disappoint them. But not when he kept his mind on being Pluto.

Of course he couldn't keep doing that every minute of the day. Who would be John Beaumont Greer then? It seemed like something he could decide to put on now and then when he needed to, the same way Pluto in the book put on his helmet and became invisible for a while. Even the god of the underworld wouldn't have worn it forever.

13

He woke up early on Sunday. It had finally cooled off and he needed to pull up the sheet. There was just enough light to make out the water stain on the wall and he thought, "This is the last morning I'll lie here looking up at that sad old lady." He lay very still so as not to waken his mama in bed across the room and watched the stain with its twisted mouth and its crazy streaming hair, trying to make it turn into something nicer, a flower or an angel, but it wouldn't. It occurred to him to ask God to do it. That would prove that God could do anything, fix anything. He closed his eyes but something about it scared him and he opened them again and wouldn't let himself look back at the wall. It wasn't right to test God.

He made up his mind to do everything exactly right that morning. He'd say something agreeable to Miss Rennie at the breakfast table, like "That sure is a pretty dress." He'd even get ready to go to church in case his daddy didn't show up beforehand. He wouldn't pack his things unless Mama told him to. He'd keep

153

acting like it was all right with him to stay on there if that was what Mama wanted. He certainly couldn't take a chance on going against his swear now.

But on his way back from the outhouse he said good morning to Bella and told her he might be going home today and seeing Pluto. "What you want me to tell him if I do?"

"Tell him I got him in my heart. But he know that. Tell him I say behave hisself and not go aggravatin' folks. If I get the chance, I make y'all some tea cakes to take along. Pluto favors my tea cakes."

"It ain't for absolutely posi*tive*ly sure we're going. Most likely we are, but don't you say I said so, all right?"

Later on after breakfast was over and after he had his good clothes on, he went into the parlor and thumbed through his grandfather's books, but he couldn't seem to set his mind to them. He got up and went over to the table in the corner where the violin lay wrapped in silky purple cloth, the violin his grandfather had loved. Gran said it was his now. He unfolded the wrapping and plinked the strings, trying for some kind of tune. The music didn't sound like much, but the violin itself was beautiful. He ran his fingers over the soft curves of golden-brown wood and lifted it carefully to his shoulder. Tucking his chin to it the way Gran had shown him, he picked up the bow and walked to where he could see himself in the mirror over the fireplace. He decided he looked just plain silly and not a bit like the important person Gran wanted him to be. The violin was very valuable, she'd said. He wondered if it would bring enough money to buy his daddy a mule. Then he thought he was crazy. While he was looking a pair of mules appeared in the mirror with him, reflected as his daddy's wagon turned into the yard. "Whoa, there. Easy now," came his daddy's voice as John laid the violin on the table and ran outside, wondering why his daddy had come in the wagon when Mama should be riding easy on the way home in the buggy Gran insisted on giving them. As soon as he saw Haze and Dancie in the wagon he knew something was wrong.

"They got Pluto," John yelled as he ran across the yard.

"What you talkin' 'bout, man?" came a familiar voice, as Pluto raised his head from the wagon bed and grinned a lopsided grin with his swollen lips. "Ain't nobody got me 'ceptin' myself." He pushed up on his elbows until his shoulders appeared over the side, then winced with pain and flopped down again.

Daddy was still in the driver's seat beside Haze, and Dancie sat beside Pluto in a low wooden chair, her own face out of shape with a purple lump beside her eye.

"Don't worry, son. It's going to be all right," Daddy said as he handed the reins to Haze and came toward John, sweeping him up in his arms so he could look down on Pluto as he lay on a pallet, not a bit all right.

His bare back was crossed with welts and Dancie swished a willow branch toward a pair of flies that had found an open cut.

"I done took right smart of a whuppin' but least-ways I ended up all in one piece," Pluto said, looking out of the corner of his eye. "How you been?"

"Just fine," he answered, numb and knowing his words didn't make any sense. "What happened?"

Daddy set him down again but hugged him up close so that a shirt button dug into John's cheek as he talked. "Seems our friend Garfield gets carried away with himself when he's got a whip in his hand. The boy's sore as a boil, but he's gonna mend. He'll be fine."

Dancie made a disgusted sound and then spit over the other side of the wagon. "Ain't gonna be fine, Mr. Joe, and you know it. Long as them nightriders be flappin' about."

"Hush up now, Dancie," Haze said. "It ain't gonna come to that. I'm gonna go tell Mama, Mr. Joe. I be right back."

"We'll be going on in a little bit, son, to take Pluto back to Treeola. Seems he destroyed some property down there and old Garfield just can't rest easy until Pluto goes back and gets what's coming to him. You stay here while I go talk to your mama for a minute."

He didn't know whether to believe his daddy. He'd said Pluto was going to be all right, but it felt like he was already dead, lying there in the wagon being dead just the way Bentley did. He felt little and cheated

156

and angry. "I don't want you going off, Plutie. I been counting on you being out yonder when I get back. I been counting on us having a heap of fun."

"You grievin' over losin' yo' play-pretty, little white boy?" Dancie asked.

"Aw, Aunt Dancie, his name be John Bo. Remember how you call him by that?"

"Things don't always go how we count on. Ain't you learnt that yet, little white boy?"

John suddenly felt ashamed of himself. Ashamed that his feelings had more to do with his own disappointment than with Pluto's future. He was a pretty sorry kind of friend. And he could see that Dancie thought the whole situation was partly his fault. Thought he ought to take some of the blame for colored people's troubles, maybe even for having white skin himself.

"I was thinking about y'all, too. I was thinking how Plutie would be a lot of company for you and Haze out there."

Dancie just looked at him. It wasn't enough.

"You think they might put him in Parchman — put him on the chain gang?" He had to know if it was going to be as bad as that.

"No tellin'. Once they gets started actin' evil, it ain't no tellin'." Her face was so hard he didn't want to look at her. Then she said, "Yo' daddy stood up to them hoodlums last night. If it hadn't of been for Mr. Joe they was ready to take off with him."

"Who was?"

"Rip Garfield and a couple of his huntin' buddies." John had never heard a colored person talk about a white man before without saying "Mister."

"That ole man had to nose around and find out how come Plutie left Treeola. Then he done made it his business to locate where he be at. Didn't take too much doin', I reckon."

"It wasn't me that told!" said John. "I didn't tell anybody anything. Not about where Plutie was staying or what happened in Treeola. Nothing. I swear I didn't." And then he added, wanting her to think he'd gone through some kind of a hard time himself, "Old Garfield talked real mean to me, but I didn't tell."

"Hey, John Bo! How 'bout you come round here to the front of the wagon so I can see you without gettin' a crick in my eyeballs, man?"

John moved up closer to the rear end of the mules than he liked to be, but now he and Pluto could get a better look at each other. Pluto lifted his chin and gave a nod. "How do? How you like my new looks?"

"You look pretty funny. Your lips are all poochy."

"Aunt Dancie's looks done changed, too. She took up for me, see? Got hit up side the head for her trouble. She a sweet lady," said Pluto, reaching out to give a pat to Dancie's bare foot.

"What was my daddy doing all that time?"

"Mr. Joe, he come home from work just 'bout the time they got to talkin' 'bout throwin' me in the Riley jailhouse. He say never mind. He say he would see to it hisself personally that I gets back to Treeola and straighten out the trouble down there. I was much obliged to him. I didn't take none to spending the night in the Riley jail."

By then, Bella was coming with Haze, her face crumpled and her cheeks wet. John remembered the look on her face the time she had said, "Pluto sho' pleasured his old granny," and the strong sure way she'd looked praying for Pluto to be taken care of. A lot of good that did. But by the time she got to the wagon the crumpled look was gone. She put her hand on Pluto's head and tipped her face up to the sky. "Praise the Lord," she said. "Thank you, Jesus, for watching over this boy." Then she reached up and lightly touched the lump by Dancie's eye and nodded slowly. Nobody said anything for what seemed like a long time, and Haze must have seen the puzzled look on John's face.

"Mama got the healin' touch, Little John. Everything be better now."

Bella took charge. "Y'all go yonder and relieve yourself at the outhouse now. You got a good long journey ahead and Miss Sally ain't gonna make no fuss about it. I fix you a little something to take along."

"No thank you, ma'am," said Dancie. "I don't have the need."

Stiffly and slowly, Pluto eased up onto his knees and then backed down out of the wagon. John felt a lot better seeing him standing up. He and Haze walked

159

with him to the back yard, and while he was inside John had the chance to ask Haze if he thought Pluto would end up on the chain gang.

"I wouldn't think so, Little John. Most likely they jest put him to work to pay for that there window."

"It cost a mighty lot. Fancy colored glass. Pluto told me all about it." He was still proud of that. "It'll probably take an awful long time to pay back for it."

"He young. He got the time."

Haze wouldn't use the outhouse after all. Said he'd just wait for the bushes by the side of the road. As they walked back to the wagon Pluto said, "John Bo, don't you give up on me now, just cause I done got sidetracked a little bit. I aim to study up on writin' so me and you can have us a newspaper printin' place like we talked about. You ain't forgot about that?"

"Shoot, no. But I got to thinking we might get more money in our pockets if we got us a barbershop instead. I hear tell there's plenty money in that and no need for fancy learning like we'd have to have for the other."

"Is that a fact? Well, I'll have to think about it. I kinda had my head set for book learnin'."

When they got to the wagon Gran was coming out of the house with a white shirt and a jar of the salve she'd put on John's toe. She thought it could cure most anything.

"Morning, everybody. Joseph tells me that crazy fool Garfield's been on a rampage. What under the sun is the matter with that man? How you feeling, Pluto?"

"I ain't none too spry this mornin', Miz Beaumont, but I reckon I be comin' along."

"Well, they can't keep a good man down, can they, boy? Here, Dancie. Put some of this on his back and cover him over with this shirt of Mr. Duff's. It's perfectly clean. Just out of the laundry basket and he'll never miss it."

"Nome," said Dancie. "Open air be good for wounds. We don't need none of that."

"Take the shirt, darlin'," said Bella, coming up with a sack of something to eat. "Too much sun ain't good for these here raw places. And all of you keep yo' eye out for mullein plants longside the road. Get a bunch of mullein leaves to lay over this child's back. You know mullein. Soft wooly leaves."

"Yessum," said Dancie, easing the shirt over Pluto.

"You mind me now and he's gonna heal up fine."

Then Mama and Papa came out, Mama bringing a jug of lemonade and her parasol for Dancie.

"We mighty sorry to hear of yo' loss, Miss Eva," said Haze.

"Why, thank you, Haze. And I feel just terrible about what happened last night. I keep telling myself if I'd never left home in the first place . . . well . . ." She gave up that line of thought and moved to the wagon. "Morning, Pluto. I'm John's mother. Now don't you try to say anything. It must hurt your poor mouth to talk. It's a shame and disgrace." Her words tumbled out. "Oh, and Dancie — just look at you," she said as Dancie turned to take the parasol from her.

"I thank you, Miss Eva. But Pluto be the one to feel for. Them mens treat that child like he was some kind of varmint got in the chicken house."

"I'd like to wring old Rip's neck for him, I'll tell you that," said Gran, "but look here. Haze can just take the wagon and drive on down there, Joseph. There's no way on earth you can get back to your job tomorrow morning, and Lord knows you can't afford to get laid off, can you?"

"Eva and I went over this, Miss Sally. I got to go. I got to see to the boy."

"Haze'll bring the wagon back. He won't run off with it, will you, Haze?"

"Miss Sally!" He'd never heard Bella sound angry at his grandmother before. "You ought to know better than that!"

"Well, now, don't get on your high horse. Just calm down. If Mr. Joe loses that job he may end up losing the whole place, and then where will Haze and Dancie be? Tell me that?"

"I have to go, Miss Sally. I gave my word."

Dancie spoke up. "We got need of him, Miz Beaumont. Them fools talkin' 'bout burnin' Plutie's mama's house if he run off again 'fo they finish up with him . . . whatever that mean. Folks down there mighty evil. You done heard what happen to Cephus, I guess. We need Mr. Joe. It just be for a day or two."

Mama put her arm around Daddy. "It's not the dratted job I'm worried about. It's you. Please be careful. Stop by on the way and get Walter to go with you. I'd feel better if your brother went along, too."

"I'll see. But there's nothing to fret about, honey. I wish to God I knew a little something about the law, but at least I can try to talk some sense to the folks stirred up over this. I'll think of something, I guess." He turned to Pluto. "Maybe I'll tell 'em what a first-rate mule handler this boy here is. Yes, siree. I'll tell 'em how I'd hire him myself in a minute if I had the mules I meant to have. I can tell 'em such as that."

John felt as proud of his father as he'd been the day he got on the locomotive train to Memphis.

"I'm coming with you, Daddy. Please. There's plenty room. All I got to do is get out of these Sunday clothes and put on my overalls. It won't take but a minute."

"Hold your horses, son. Nothing doing. I can't take you along. And you know why?"

"No, sir."

"Because if I did, who's gonna drive Mama home in the buggy in time to milk Betsy and feed the chickens and let poor old Lucy out of the corn crib where we had to shut her up this morning? Think you could handle all that?"

"Yessir," he said, dazed by the good mixed in with so much bad. "We'll get on home. I can take care of everything."

"Well, then. I'm coming, too," said Gran. "Eva's not right yet. I'm not about to let her stay out yonder with nobody but this child."

Daddy hugged Mama good-bye. "Be careful, sweetheart," she whispered.

Gran shook her head. "Joseph, I hope you know what you're doing."

"We'll find out in time, Miss Sally. And I want you to know I appreciate how you been looking after my wife for me."

"Looking after my flesh and blood doesn't call for thank-yous from anybody." John moved away from his grandmother because he had a strong urge to kick her.

"Well," said Daddy, reaching over to rumple John's hair, "I aim to take her off your hands now."

Gran pulled Mama back toward her a little. "Best let him go, daughter. Y'all get along now so you'll be there well before night. And look out for one another." Everybody got in.

"You a good man, Mr. Joe," said Bella. "Pluto, you do what he say and tell yo' mama I'm gonna come when I can."

John ran along by the wagon as it picked up speed. "There's a whole heap I meant to tell you about, Plutie. I didn't get to say hardly any of it. Hey, I learned all about your name, for one thing!"

"Write me a letter, man. I figure it out some way."

"I'll come see you if they put you in Parchman. It ain't too far to come once they let me start riding." His legs were about to give out now and his words came in gasps as he ran. "And I wanted to — talk some more about having us a barbershop — or whatever."

"Ain't gonna happen, white boy. Ain't never gonna happen," came Dancie's sharp voice. He stopped finally and watched the wagon move away from him. "Bye, y'all," he called. He was pretty sure they couldn't tell he was crying. Pluto's hand waved over the side of the wagon. Dancie raised the parasol and held it over Pluto and waved, too. "Take care of yo'self, John Bo," she called.

14

When he got back Jesse had come with Maud to hitch up the buggy, but he didn't hang around after he finished. Mama and Gran took off for church without making a fuss because he wouldn't go. He changed into his overalls and, emptying the bureau drawer onto the bed, he folded his clothes very carefully and stacked them in a pile. They were going home all right, and it was nothing like he'd thought it would be. Pluto wasn't going to be there. No telling what was going to happen to him. If Daddy lost his job they'd probably have to come back here anyhow. If this was the way God answered prayers he just might not ever do a speck of praying again. Giving you a little something you ask for and then snatching away so much else. Seemed like that was all God was good for. Just taking away one thing after another. Brothers, Daddy's mule money, Mama's new baby, and now Pluto. He never should have put so much stock in that praying Bella did. For the first time he let it come clear in his mind that she probably prayed for Pluto's brother, too. For Cephus when he was in Parchman. He was her grandson, too, same as Pluto. But look what happened to him.

When he had finished folding all the clothes he stood in the middle of the room not knowing what to do next. He couldn't be still. He had too many jangly feelings. But at the same time his feet felt too heavy to move and he couldn't think where to go anyhow.

"I'll skin him alive," Mr. Garfield had said. John wondered if the feeling in his stomach meant he might be going to throw up. He'd better not throw up all over his stack of clothes. Maybe he ought to move around some. He couldn't decide. Then he noticed the sewing scissors Mama had been using, and it came to him what he was going to do. He slid the blades into his overall pocket and left by the front door.

When he got to the livery stable his legs were shaking, but he walked on in and said he'd been sent with a message for Jesse. He went straight on back without waiting for anybody to tell him he could. It was easy enough to tell by his haircut which one was Henry, and after he gave him a handful of clover he had picked on the way, he snipped off what was left of the mule's stubbly mane before anybody noticed what he was up to. Then he climbed over the fence and went home.

He ran all the way and collapsed on the back steps, sobbing now and out of breath. Bella came out of the garden where she'd been picking tomatoes for dinner and eased herself down beside him. She put her hand on his shoulder, rubbing it a little, without saying a word. Nobody but Lucy had ever seen him cry hard like that before. When he quieted down after a while, he'd stopped feeling like his insides were going to explode. The two of them sat there being still and sad together.

"Praying didn't do any good," he said finally.

"Oh, well now, I wouldn't say that. Pluto ain't thrivin' right now, but he sho is alive and that's a mercy."

"He won't come back. Maybe not ever."

"Maybe not. We can't hold on to folks the way we wants to. That ain't easy to learn."

"Here we are going home, but I wanted him to be there. All it's gonna be is lonesome. We been talking about doing a lot of stuff together, not just now but later on. Dancie says it can't ever happen. Not ever."

"Dancie don't know everything."

"I'm giving up on church," he said. He knew it was a terrible thing to say, but he didn't care.

"Seem to me, John Beaumont, you got it all wrong about prayin'. Listen here. What you do is you takes yo' troubles to the Lord. That's the right way. Tell Him yo' grief. But then don't you go on and try to tell Him every little thing to do about it. Me and you ain't got eyes enough in our head to run the world on our say-so. We think we know how to fix it all, we got another think comin'."

"You prayed for Cephus, too, though, didn't you, that time?"

"Yes, I did. That I did. No way I ever coulda gone on lessen I took that burden to the Lord."

"Well, it was awful, and God didn't do anything about it. But somebody sure ought to." He remembered how Pluto had answered when he'd said the very same words to him, looking at him like he was a dummy to say such a thing — "And who you think that gonna be?"

Bella hummed to herself for a while and then said, "For all we know, child, the Lord could be doin' something unbeknownst this minute. Could be workin' inside some little chilluns who gonna grow up thinkin' it ain't right the way things is. Thinkin' it don't have to stay just like that for everlastin'."

They were quiet some more after that, and then John said, "I sure hope I recollect what Haze told me about milking Betsy. I was having trouble getting the hang of it."

"I speck you gonna manage. You find the way to do what you have to do. Goodness knows ole Betsy gonna have to be milked."

"Maybe I'll go write Plutie a letter. You could take it to him when you go down there, couldn't you?"

"I don't see why not."

He started the letter off, "We could raise mules or run a barbershop or have us a newspaper, whichever one you pick." Then he told about what the *Laurel*

Library said, making a few changes so it would be easier for somebody just figuring out how to read. "I been looking up about the old-timey God of the Underworld you got your name from and like you said, he was mighty powerful. He ruled over all the dead people there ever was and that's a mighty lot of folks. He was a heap richer than all the other gods on account of being in charge of every speck of the gold and jewels hidden down deep in the ground, probably even the rubies in that old red-eyed owl. One special thing he had was a kind of cap called a helmet he could put on his head when he didn't want anybody to see him and nobody could. What you better figure out right quick is how to get you one like that. From your good buddy, John Bo."

At the top of the page, so he'd know right off that the letter was meant for him, he wrote, "Pluto Johnson can write good." Pluto already knew all the letters in that sentence. They made up more than half the alphabet. Even if they did lock him up in Parchman and send him out to chop cotton with chains on his ankles, he'd make it his business to learn the rest of the letters somehow. And one day he'd send an answer back.

John could hear Mama and Gran coming home. He still had something else to do, so he scooted out the back of the house and disappeared through the crepe myrtle bushes along the alleyway. He went on down to where the brick schoolhouse sat. The playing yard was empty. Boys were probably changing out of their good clothes now that church was over, and once they'd had their dinner they'd be all over the place, playing ball, yelling and making fun of the ones they didn't like.

He stood looking at the big building, letting the scared feeling from it swarm over him. He narrowed his eyes. It still looked like a fierce red bull to him, but he spread out his elbows and fingers and went at it in the same kind of monster walk Pluto had used at the angry mother hen the first time John saw him. Then he straightened up and took a deep breath. Maybe he'd be riding in on a mule, or maybe he'd end up coming to stay at his grandmother's. But one way or another he was going to go to this school and get himself a really good education. It didn't matter that his knees would be knocking like crazy when he walked up those steps, that he didn't know enough, that he was scared and a worrywart. Pluto had probably been plenty scared lots of times, scared really bad last night and other times, too.

John imagined what his friend might say if he was standing here. "Legs," he'd say, "you may be shakin', but that ain't gonna get you out of goin' on about yo' business. You can make it up them steps. And that ain't all. Once I finish up here, you gonna step onto that locomotive train so I can ride up to Memphis and learn a whole heap more. We got a mighty lot to figure out."

Then he said the same thing all over again. Well, it was almost the same thing, but it came out different

171

because he said it being John Beaumont Greer that time instead of Pluto, and it made him feel good. Full of himself. It was funny, that was what Gran used to say when she meant he was acting too big for his britches. "Watch out," she'd say. "You're getting too full of yourself." But that was how it felt now and it felt good.

He walked on home, taking his time, figuring if he happened to run into Daisy and her mama on the way he might could talk them into buying an encyclopedia. The blue jay feather was still in his pocket. He figured maybe he'd go back and watch those boys playing ball after dinner, if there was time before he drove his mama home.